"If you marry me you'll share my bed—and no one else's."

Tamara straightened. "You make that sound like a command."

But the sparks firing over her skin weren't entirely from indignation. True, part of her shrank from the idea of sleeping with a man she barely knew. Yet another, more secret part...

As if reading her mind, he nudged closer. "The idea of consummating our marriage...worries you?"

Suddenly an image of his mouth claiming hers came to mind. A drugging heat seeped through her, and her eyes drifted closed.

This was too intense. Too *soon*.

She turned a tight circle to face him—or rather the wall of his chest. Steeling herself, she shouldered past him. "Don't get ahead of yourself, *Mr De Luca*..."

Robyn Grady left a fifteen-year career in television production, knowing that the time was right to pursue her dream of writing romance. She adores cats, clever movies, and spending time with her wonderful husband and their three precious daughters. Living on Australia's glorious Sunshine Coast, her perfect day includes a beach, a book, and no laundry when she gets home.

Robyn loves to hear from readers. You can contact her at www.robyngrady.com

THE MAGNATE'S MARRIAGE DEMAND

BY
ROBYN GRADY

MILLS & BOON®
Pure reading pleasure™

First published in Great Britain 2009
Harlequin Mills & Boon Limited,
Eton House, 18-24 Paradise Road, Richmond, Surrey TW9 1SR

© Robyn Grady 2007

ISBN: 978 0 263 87197 5

Set in Times Roman 10½ on 13 pt
01-0409-43979

Printed and bound in Spain
by Litografia Rosés, S.A., Barcelona

THE MAGNATE'S MARRIAGE DEMAND

Melissa Jeglinski, for believing in my book
and her continued encouragement and guidance.

Karen Solem, my 'super agent.'

Tessa Radley, a friend indeed.

Rachel Robinson, Melissa James and Gail Fuller,
my incredible CPs.

CHAPTER ONE

TAMARA KENDLE couldn't seem to keep her eyes off the darkly attractive man who sat alone in the chapel's front pew—he was like a rock, unmoving, staring dead ahead.

Guilt pricked each time her attention wavered from the minister at the lectern. She was here to say goodbye to someone special. A person she missed so much, her heart physically ached. She felt clobbered, stuck somewhere between reality and hell.

And yet, to the left of the rosewood casket and waterfalls of perfumed lilies, broad-jacketed shoulders continued to intrigue. Though they hadn't met in person, Tamara knew the man by more than reputation.

Armand De Luca, Australia's multimillionaire steel magnate, the last of his bloodline.

Or so he thought.

Tamara had already been seated when De Luca had entered the funeral home chapel. Throughout the service the classic lines of his profile had exuded the confidence men admire and women fall immediately in love with. Square-cut jaw, well-proportioned nose and lips, those eyes…high noon blue, heavy-lidded, yet all-knowing.

"Thank you all for attending." Tamara's attention slid back to the minister; a solemn smile alleviated his long thin face. "There will be a wake in the adjoining building for those who wish to come together and remember Marc Earle."

Tamara crossed herself, recited a private prayer, then eased out a defeated sigh. Marc had been her dearest friend. They'd laughed together, confided in each other. And a few months ago, when a string of unfortunate events had threatened to pull her under…

Tears prickled and stung her eyes.

God knew she was a fighter. Growing up, she had to be. But that night she'd needed someone and, as always, Marc had been there.

As Tamara pushed to her feet, an icy shiver trickled down her spine. While others shuffled into the aisle, up ahead Armand De Luca was crossing the maroon carpet, headed for the casket. His face a stony mask, he gazed down then reached out to touch the gleaming wood.

A wave of nausea surged in Tamara's belly. Sweeping aside her long dark hair, she closed her eyes, gently pressing a hand below her waist. She breathed all the way in, then slowly out. When the morning sickness faded, she looked over again. De Luca was gone.

Suddenly chilled, she hugged herself then followed the majority's lead, drifting through ethereal shafts of light that crisscrossed down from parallel arched windows. Outside, she slid on dark glasses to shield her gritty eyes from a screen of mostly nameless faces that milled around like ghosts slow-waltzing to receding organ music.

Two of Marc's friends gravitated over. Identical in every way but their hair, twins Kristin and Melanie had often called upon their kind-hearted neighbor to help with handyman chores or settle sibling squabbles. Now the pair looked lost.

Kristin slowly shook her cropped blond head. "I'm still in shock." Her brows flew together. "I told him not to get that stupid motorbike."

Melanie's rust-colored locks quivered when she blew her nose. "This should never have happened to someone as good as Marc." She sighed then blinked at Tamara. "Can't imagine how you're coping. With your business going under, then the fire, now this."

While Tamara struggled to form words, Kristin snapped at her sister. "Great going, Mel. She doesn't need reminders."

"I only meant that three knocks in a row…" Melanie looked sheepish. "Well, it must be tough."

Three knocks?

Tamara swayed.

Make that four.

Others joined the trio. Half-listening, Tamara stared off at the distant cityscape sprawled below the funeral home's high vantage point. The glass-and-metal structures, poised like sentinels around Sydney Harbor's stretched-silk waters, normally charged her with energy and excitement. None of that registered today.

When her queasiness grew and mourners meandered off toward a room where triangular sandwiches, hot tea and more anguish awaited, she slipped away to the nearest bathroom. Moments later, she clutched the comfortless rim of a porcelain sink.

Oh, Lord, she was going to be sick. But at least she was alone in the private room available for anyone who needed time to gather their thoughts or composure. Bowed over, brow embedded on a forearm, she submitted to rolls of discomfort and the image that spun an endless cycle through her brain—Marc's face the night he'd learned he would soon be a father. He'd said that he loved her. Wanted to get married. How could she confess she loved him too—just not that way.

The scent of pine antiseptic and freshly cut gladioli hauled her back. A heartbeat later, her ears pricked and she straightened. Had she heard something—a knock?

She slumped again. No, just ragged nerves and imagination. Groaning, she cupped shaking hands under the running faucet. Another splash on her clammy face could only help.

"Excuse me, Ms. Kendle?"

At the sound of that rich, honey-over-gravel voice, Tamara's heart jumped to her throat. Hair lashing her cheeks, she wheeled around to face the room's only exit and the masculine silhouette filling it. Palm pushed to the pounding beneath the bodice of her black dress, she swallowed and recovered her power of speech. "Good Lord, you scared me half to death!"

One dark brow flexed as an indolent grin kicked up a corner of her guest's mouth. "My apologies. When you slid in here, and stayed so long, I worried that I'd missed you." Beneath the impeccably tailored jacket, his sizeable chest inflated. "I'm Armand De Luca. Marco's brother."

Long-lost brother, she silently amended, though it was apparent they had nothing in common, not manner or build. And while Marc's eyes were blue, too, his gaze had been trusting, whereas this man's appeared, well, almost predatory. Perhaps not so surprising given what she knew of his upbringing. A strict childhood, dominated by an overly ambitious father, no mother on the scene. She might feel sorry for him, but De Luca was not a man in need of pity. Ruthless intelligence and celebrated charm, which radiated off him now in tangible waves, was proof enough of that.

Tamara sucked down a cleansing breath and, cutting off the faucet's flow, found a polite smile. "Marc spoke of you."

He smiled. "I'm glad. I'd hoped you and I could talk now."

He held her eyes, his expression amicable yet potent, and some unknown impulsive part of her felt compelled to nod and agree. But a lengthy conversation was out of the question. Not today, in any case. Not when she felt ready to collapse. When her world had all but collapsed around her.

She tore paper from the chrome-plated dispenser to blot her hands. "It's been an exhausting day, but I'm sure others would love the chance to talk with you about Marc."

"I don't have a lot of time, Ms. Kendle. I wish only to speak with you."

She tossed the paper wad into a nearby bin, her smile strained and curious now. "That sounds rather ominous."

"Marco said you were bright."

Her heartbeat stuttered, not only at his words, but also his gaze, probing, analyzing, as if he were hunting out her most precious secret. As if he somehow suspected the news she wasn't quite yet ready to share.

Expression cool, she collected her purse from the vanity and slung its strap over a shoulder. Truth told, he intimidated her, but damned if she'd let him know.

She met his gaze square on. "You don't look the type to play games. So tell me, what's this all about?"

He regarded her for a long moment then stepped from the slanted shadows of the doorway into the room's harsh artificial light. A subtle widow's peak complemented his high brow. Above a strong, stubborn jaw, unyielding brackets framed a masculine yet sensually sculptured mouth. Armand De Luca wasn't merely attractive. He possessed raw animal magnetism barely contained beneath a highly polished air. The overall effect went beyond arresting. It was downright dangerous.

A pulse jumped in his jaw. "You're pregnant," he stated, "with Marco's child."

His announcement winded her like a blow to the stomach. Her knees threatened to buckle as questions pummeled her brain. Morning sickness had taken a firm hold, but she wasn't showing yet. Did De Luca own a crystal ball?

She narrowed her eyes. "How can you know? I only told Marc an hour before the accident."

His impassive expression didn't change. "He rang to

share the news. Since our reunion, my younger brother occasionally kept in touch."

Tamara didn't know much about their history, other than their parents had separated when the boys were quite young. Marc never said why his mother had taken him but not Armand when she'd left, or why as adults the brothers hadn't been in touch until after their father's death over a year ago. Marc never wallowed in the past, another reason she'd respected him. Emotional baggage, skeletons in the closet…it dragged a person down and dredged up doubts, if revisited too often.

Yet today Marc's past had caught up with the present while Tamara's future grew safe and treasured inside of her.

Maternal pride lifted her chin. "Yes, I'm pregnant. But there's no need to track me down like this. I'm not leaving the country."

"I am. My jet departs for Beijing in a few hours. I'll be gone two weeks."

She forced a cordial smile. "Then we'll talk in two weeks."

As she finished the sentence, an idea struck. She had nothing keeping her in Sydney. Perhaps he was worried she'd disappear, not caring if he saw the baby, his little niece or nephew. The last thing she wanted was to cut him from her child's life as he had once been cut from Marc's. She knew how destructive those kinds of divisions could be.

Her greatest wish was to give her child a happy, balanced home. That meant one day marrying the man who loved them both and whom she loved in return, not merely as a friend, but as a wife should love her husband. More immediately, however, her baby's interests would be best served by including extended family.

Her expression softened. "Look, if you're concerned about visits, please don't be. I want my child to know his uncle. Family is important." She hesitated, then confessed, "More important than anything."

The line between his brows eased even while he appeared otherwise unaffected. "Please, share five minutes with me, Ms. Kendle, away from here."

The dark edge to his voice, that shiver racing through her blood...

She hadn't been certain before, but these last few seconds she felt it as surely as the hair rising on the back of her neck. Something was very wrong.

Her heartbeat slowed then thudded low in her chest. Was there a hereditary disease she needed to know about? Epilepsy, allergies, heart conditions...some problem that might need immediate attention?

Her throat closed around a lump as her head prickled hot and cold. "Whatever this is about, if it concerns the child I'm carrying, I want to know." She swallowed hard. "And I want to know now."

One large tanned hand flexed by his side before he drew up tall and gradually closed the distance separating them, 'til her senses swam with his hot, woodsy scent and she couldn't escape the resolve hardening in his eyes.

"It does concern the child, Ms. Kendle, as well as both of us." De Luca's broad shoulders squared. "I want to marry you."

* * *

Fifteen minutes later, Armand sat with one arm slung over the back of a shaded park bench, Tamara Kendle in a daze at his side. Despite the salty breeze lifting the hair off her cheek, her face looked whiter than the styrene cup her delicate hand clutched. Jaw slack, she stared at an endless procession of waves, which crashed and ebbed on the foam-scalloped shore a few meters away.

Clearly she was still in shock. When he'd let loose his bombshell proposal at the funeral home earlier, her legs had given way. He'd swooped to catch her and in the instant her warm body had slumped against his, damned if his blood hadn't sparked and caught light. Then had come a blinding flash of guilt.

That guilt burned low in his gut now, but he clenched his jaw and pushed it aside. He'd seen Marco exactly eight times in the last fourteen months, including the re-introduction at their father's funeral. Now the brother he'd barely known was dead.

Marrying the woman Marco had loved might sound insensitive, perhaps even shameless to some. Armand understood the sentiment but he wouldn't let that color his decision. He played by his own rules, no one else's. To wish things were somehow different was useless. Nothing changed the past, there was only the future, and a union would benefit them all—Tamara, the baby, as well as himself.

Easing out a breath, Armand leaned forward. Forearms resting on thighs, he dropped his threaded hands between his knees. "Would you like more water or are you okay to talk?"

The timing was worse than bad. If that issue in China

weren't calling him out of the country, he'd have approached this differently and merely introduced himself today, following it up with visits over the next few days until she felt more comfortable. Although their meeting was awkward, perhaps it was better this way. Much needed to be organized—and quickly—particularly the effects of a betrothal upon his business and late father's legal trust.

With great care, Tamara set the cup on a slat between them and looped stray hair behind an ear. "If you want to talk about weddings, there's nothing to say."

As the information filtered through, he saw suspicion pool in her eyes and renewed tension ratchet back her shoulders.

"My…situation?"

His tone was nonconfrontational, yet firm. "You've been out of work two months, since your business failed to trade out of cash flow problems."

"Thanks to a big company that refused to pay an invoice." Uncertainty furrowed her brows. "How did you know? Marc wouldn't have told you. It had nothing to do with you."

"Now it does." He met her glistening gaze, green eyes filled with shifting light.

He rubbed his bristled jaw, laid his arm along the back of the bench again and set his thoughts on track. "You don't have private insurance."

She blinked as if the idea hadn't occurred to her. "No, I don't."

"But you'd obviously want the best doctor to care for you and the baby." She sank back, her pallor even more pasty. "What about the delivery? If you need a caesarean, don't you want to know who's holding the knife?"

"We have a good public system in this country."

"You know where and who you'd want to care for the baby, and it's not waiting hours in a medical clinic, seeing a different, overworked doctor every time." He passed on a jaded look. "In today's triage world, if you want to be certain of having the best, you need to pay for it."

Her pointed gaze skewered his. "I'll ask again. How do you know all this?"

He shrugged. "A few phone calls." The best medical care wasn't the only thing money could buy. By comparison, information was cheap.

Her cheeks flamed red as a volcano built inside of her—again, not unexpected.

"You had me investigated?"

"I looked in to my late brother's affairs."

"You mean his love affair."

He tipped closer and willed her to understand. This wasn't pleasant for him, either. "You have no income and no family to speak of. I want to help."

"By proposing marriage. Isn't that a bit extreme? What about something simple, like writing a check?" She crossed her arms and tucked in that cute cleft chin. "Not that I want your money."

"That's noble, but in your predicament, perhaps impractical."

Although by no means wealthy, Marco had been in more of a position to reject the De Luca legacy, even laugh off the suggestion that the brothers might finally unite and build together. Tamara's situation was somewhat different.

Mottled pink consumed her neck. "I'm more than capable of holding down a job."

"Like being a receptionist at your local budget hairdressers." Her jaw dropped. "You'll be up and down, sweeping floors, helping out, on your feet eight to ten hours a day. From what I saw of you bent over that sink, early pregnancy doesn't agree with you. How will you cope?"

Pride pinned back her shoulders. Despite her stubbornness, he had to admire her. An educated guess said if anyone could make it through this difficult situation on her own and do it well, she could. But he'd keep that to himself.

"I'm grateful for the job, even if it is a stopgap," she told him. "I plan to finish a business degree then relaunch my special events company." She tilted her head and conceded, "Or, if need be, I'll take a position with another firm and work my way up." She sent him an almost impish look. "But you might already know that, too."

His mouth twitched. Minx. Quite a change from the gushing society princesses he'd dated—women of a mold who flattered, simpered and left him tepid, as far as sweethearts or long-term relationships were concerned.

Ah, who was he kidding? He didn't believe in romantic love and hadn't for some time, though clearly others did.

He studied a patch of sandy ground, searching for the right words. "I know you and Marco were in love. He said you were going to marry and have more children. Obviously it will take time to recover from your loss—"

"Whoa! Hold on." Tamara waved her hands. "Marc might have been in love with me, but I hadn't agreed to marry him. I thought of him only as a friend. A very dear friend."

Armand froze. Every muscle, every thought locked in black ice. Finally he raked a hand through his hair. He wasn't a saint, but this idea refused to compute. "Do you often sleep with friends, Ms. Kendle?"

She jerked back as if slapped. Grabbing her bag, she shot to her feet. "I've heard enough."

As she spun on her heel, he snared her arm. They weren't finished yet.

He hauled her back. The skin-to-skin contact jolted a physical response that pumped through his arteries, scorching his flesh, just as it had an hour ago when he'd proposed and she'd buckled against him. Completely aware, he slowly stood and tried to absorb this sensation's deeper meaning. From her startled gaze, she felt it, too—that current, popping and pulsing like a live wire between them.

His gaze skimmed a hot line over her lips as a dormant beast yawned and stretched inside him. "You weren't sexually attracted to Marco?"

Yet an unmistakable attraction simmered between the two of them. For obvious reasons, he hadn't expected this. Didn't quite know what to do with it—a first for him, in many ways.

Regaining control, she shrugged out of his grasp. "Marc was kind and thoughtful and put everything on hold if a friend needed him. It happened once." Her bruised heart sat like a shadow in her eyes. "I don't expect you to understand."

His chest burned, but he pushed ahead. He had no time to dwell on who the better man had been.

"You've had a bad run." He knew about her house and the fire, too. "But today you have an opportunity to turn things around."

A hapless smile twisted her mouth. "A marriage of convenience?" The open vulnerability, the innocence of her face, worked to find a way under his ribs and he nodded once. She seemed to digest the sincerity of his offer before fresh wariness dawned in her eyes. "What's in it for you?"

He didn't hesitate. "This child will have two parents."

She waited. "And?"

"You need another reason?"

Tamara Kendle came from a broken home, one far less privileged than his own had been. An absent father and uneducated mother. Tamara's childhood made his gripes look like too little cake at a Sunday picnic. Surely the security in providing this child a decent family life should be persuasion enough.

A clutch of grounded seagulls scattered as she left him to wander toward the beach fence. The breeze, stronger here, combed her hair, turning it to dark ribbons that danced down her back.

She rotated to face him, her expression perceptive now. "You said I was bright, Mr. De Luca. Please don't dodge my question."

After a moment, he exhaled and joined her. Resting both palms on the chest-high railing, he perused the rolling sea. "Yes, there is another reason." She'd need to know anyway.

She propped one elbow on the railing and cupped her cheek. "I'm listening."

He clenched the wood. "I need to obtain the controlling interest in my late father's company. His will left the balance in trust."

"And I fit in how…?"

"A stipulation must be met before the interest can revert to me. I must produce offspring—a child—by my thirty-third birthday. In other words, I need a legitimate heir seven months from now."

"My baby?" A disbelieving laugh escaped. "Can people actually do that in their wills? It sounds medieval."

"Dante, my father, was very much old guard. I'd known for years he wanted to ensure that his legacy continued through me into the next generation." His jaw shifted as he rationalized. "It's understandable."

"And if you don't produce an heir by the deadline?"

"The controlling interest will remain with my father's closest friend, the company's legal advisor."

A man with no children of his own. Someone Armand had admired and called uncle growing up. A person he trusted and whom he believed would pass on the balance anyway. But he'd rather comply with his father's wishes, and, in doing so, avoid placing Matthew, an ethical man, in a not-so-ethical position. Convincing Tamara to marry him would eliminate those glitches and lead to a win-win situation for everyone, including the child.

She looked skeptical. "This doesn't add up. A man like you would have zero problems finding a more than willing bride. Why leave it 'til now?"

He refused to feel. Refused to remember. Instead he twirled the heavy ruby ring on his right hand. "Let's just say, true love has eluded me."

"You want to find true love?"

The visible tension in her jaw eased before she slowly straightened and gave in to her first real smile. The expression was like a candle flickering to life on the inside, making her glow like an angel. He almost smiled back.

"Then you'd understand why this can't possibly work," she said. "Why you'll have to find another way. I want to find that right one, too, just like you."

He studied her. She was far more attractive than he'd first thought, with creamy skin, long regal neck and a small gold cross shining from the hollow of her throat. And for a cock-eyed moment, he wanted to steal some of her starry-eyed enthusiasm. But he'd tossed believing a long time ago.

Prying his gaze from the curve of her cheek, he focused again on the sea. "You misunderstand. I don't believe in fairy tales."

She fell back against the fence, emitting a soft gasp. "You mean you don't believe in love?"

He bit down, suddenly irritated, but nevertheless well-versed for the argument. Not that this discussion need include an analysis of his personal regrets; he took as his right the discretion of one mistake. He would stick to broader statistics.

"I have a friend who's a divorce lawyer, but it's no secret. Half the people who marry for love separate. That's compared to four percent of arranged marriages. In some parts of the world, such betrothals are considered a privilege."

She blinked twice. "Good Lord, you're serious."

"What I propose is a partnership built on honesty and respect."

"What you propose is out of the question!"

He held up a hand. "I understand it's not the best time."

"Darn right it's not. Your brother was buried today." She backed up, disgust dragging on her mouth. "And, whatever you might believe, I'm not a piece of property you can buy to better your business standing, and neither is my baby. Yes, I want honesty and respect from the man I marry. But I also want a history and commitment and passion."

Her green eyes were all sparks and fire now, all conviction and courage. No interest in material gain…only ideals. "Passion?" he asked, all the more curious.

Her eyes widened as if she'd read his thoughts and wasn't sure how to take them. "Every woman wants that."

His gaze roamed her face. "Most men, too."

He didn't make choices lightly. He'd lain awake last night and had sat in that chapel today analyzing the pros and cons of marrying a woman he'd yet to meet in order to fulfill the terms of the will and give her child—his blood—the De Luca name. Yet, not once had Armand anticipated this pull, the impulse to frame her face and test her warmth.

The tug in his chest, the heat down below…

Hell. He wanted to kiss her.

She broke their gaze. Combing back hair that waved like a pennant across her face, she looked down at her feet, then over to the busy road. She still avoided his eyes when she said, "You have a plane waiting and I need to go home and get over this day."

He snatched a glance at his watch. Damn. Where had that hour gone? But he still had time. He'd make time. "I'll give you a lift."

He reached for her elbow, but she weaved away. "I'll take the bus. I mean it," she insisted when he began to protest. While he reluctantly stepped back, she seemed to gather her thoughts. "I also meant what I said about not excluding you from our lives." After a hesitant moment, she fished around in her purse. "I suppose you already have my phone number."

The tension, which had locked his shoulder blades these past few days, eased slightly. He did have her number, but he wouldn't object if she gave it to him. She was giving him an inch. For now, that was all he needed.

After she'd retrieved a notepad and pen, his gaze settled on the motion of her writing…left-handed, skin smooth, fingers long and slender, made for jewelry. Diamonds, emeralds, maybe even rubies.

She handed him the paper, shot out a quick goodbye and was gone, swift as a frightened hare. Watching her move through the shade of bobbing palm fronds toward a bus stop, he shifted his weight to one leg and scratched his temple. Fourteen days and nights in China suddenly seemed like a very long time.

Walking to his car, Armand opened her note. He stopped in his tracks to read the message three times.

Give me some space!

His grin was slow. He'd give her two weeks. After that, he couldn't promise anything.

CHAPTER TWO

Tamara trudged in through her apartment's paint-flaked doorway, holding her wrist, fighting tears of pain and frustration.

For six days she had rushed around at the salon, most of the time on her feet. She'd battled constant morning sickness and had graciously accepted the pitiful wage. But a collision with a fellow employee, which had left her wrist swollen and sore, was the final straw. After writing her resignation and a twenty-minute walk home, she was done in—too exhausted to think, too tired to care. An earthquake could shake the continent and she just might sleep through it.

Her purse dropped with a thud near the bedroom door. After kicking off her flats, she dug a bag of green peas from the ancient freezer and ripped the tea towel from its kitchen rack. With both wrapped around her throbbing wrist, she sank horizontally into the worn velour couch.

She was drifting when the phone buzzed.

Throwing her good hand over her eyes, she groaned. "Not interested. Go away."

But it could be the employment agency. She might want to crash for a month, but that was a luxury she couldn't afford.

Pushing up, she brushed the stack of overdue bills aside and rescued the side table handset.

Melanie's voice chirped on the line. "Me and Kristen wondered how you were doing. It's been over a week. Guess it's finally sinking in, huh?"

Tamara wedged back into the lumpy cushions and stared at the ceiling. One benefit to being busy and exhausted—she hadn't been able to mire herself in the depths of grief. Marc was gone; yes, it was sinking in, and she would miss him more than anyone could know. As head of her own company, she'd projected an outgoing personality, but at heart she was shy.

At twenty-six her natural bent was still to do it alone. But she'd felt so comfortable, so herself whenever she'd been with Marc. That was one of the reasons he'd been so special to her and why the baby would mean even more.

She patted the white cotton shirt where she imagined her secret bump had begun to grow. "Thanks for calling, Mel. I'm doing okay." Her gaze slid to her university textbooks, stacked in a neat pile on the gray Formica table. She coiled one leg around the other, bare foot tucked behind the opposite jean-clad knee, and turned her back. She wasn't ready to face that challenge just now.

"What about you guys?" she asked. "Keeping out of trouble?"

While Melanie summarized their week—a weepie movie, two new hairstyles—Tamara forced herself to thumb through the bills: a reminder utility notice threatening disconnection and a warning in ugly red letters announcing rent was two weeks late. She wondered how they evicted people these days. Would she be marched out by the scruff of her neck?

A booming rap on the door echoed through the room. Her breath caught and the bill crunched in her hand.

Melanie paused. "Something wrong?"

Stomach sinking, Tamara eased to her feet. "Just the door. I'll call back."

If this was the landlord ready to toss her out, no use delaying it. There were always the options of government benefits, or cheaper accommodation. She looked around the matchbox room. Was there anything cheaper than this?

The bell rang next, long and shrill. Ironing back frazzled wisps that escaped from her waist-length ponytail, Tamara moved one foot in front of the other. After touching the cross at her throat, she yanked on the handle and her heart exploded through her chest.

First thing she noticed was dark trousers sheathing long masculine legs like a work of art. Next, an open-necked business shirt, cuffs folded back on hard, bronzed forearms. Higher, stubble smudged a movie-star square jaw, while a lick of black hair hung over a widow's peak. The gaze was blue, lazy and hypnotic.

Armand De Luca.

Partway recovered, she exhaled in a whoosh. "I thought you said two weeks."

He hinted at a smile. "Turned into one."

Still off balance, she rested a cheek against her fingers, which were curled around the door rim, and surrendered to the obvious. "Don't tell me. You've already heard."

His expression sharpened. "Let me guess. You've tossed in your salon receptionist towel." His attention zeroed in on the wrapped bag of peas pinioned against her lower ribs and he frowned. "I can also see why." Without invitation, he crossed the threshold and gingerly collected her injured hand.

Her first impulse was to twist away, tell him to keep his distance. She wasn't at all certain she welcomed what his touch did to her—like being sucked in by the tow of a tidal wave. But she was so tired; avoiding his hands-on concern only seemed childish. Besides, his big tanned hand supporting her much smaller one wasn't exactly unpleasant.

"I'd invite you in—" she watched him untangle the towel, then gently roll her wrist back and forth "—but you already are."

His focus was on the swollen joint. "This looks bad."

The hot pad of his index finger nudged the purple mark, which was turning greenish-yellow, and a searing pain lifted the hair on her scalp. Water flooding her eyes, she broke free of his hold and moved toward the couch, cradling her wrist like a baby.

Rubbing a set of knuckles over his sandpaper jaw, he followed. "That needs to be looked at."

"It just needs rest."

He took her in, from her muzzy ponytail to her naked toes, and sent a disapproving look that made her feel ten years old. "*You* need rest."

Bingo! "You're right. So if you don't mind…" She

made to crowd him back out the door, but she had more chance of moving Ayres Rock. For now, she was beaten.

She pasted on a plastic smile, not intending to hide her frustration. "So, what can I do for you today, Mr. De Luca?"

His voice deepened, part velvet, part growl. "It's Armand. And you can come home with me."

His statement pushed her back with the force of a shove. But she wouldn't give him the satisfaction of seeing how much his words, and presence, affected her.

Her grin was haughty. "Persistence must be your middle name. 'Come home with me,' just like that." She fell back into the couch. Her wrist screamed and she yelped at the pain.

His athletic frame folded down beside her. The ledge of his broad shoulders swung over and the room seemed to shrink. "Not just like that. Not only are you injured, you're forgetting our conversation last week."

Too aware of his animal magnetism and intoxicating woodsy scent, she slid farther away. "I haven't forgotten anything." Including the fact he'd approached her with that ludicrous offer of marriage at Marc's funeral.

He looked past her and frowned. Oh, great. He'd spotted the bills. When he swept them up—an obstinate man with a mission—more than instinct said it was a waste of time to protest. She assumed an unconcerned air while her heartbeat clattered wildly.

Finally he set the bills down. "Do you have anywhere to go?"

She forced a laugh. The sound came out more strangled than amused. "It's not as bad as all that."

His bland expression let her know he didn't agree.

As tense seconds ticked by, the walls pressed in, and as much as it pained her, Tamara was forced to face the hard, cold truth. Aside from Marc, she didn't have anyone close. Melanie and Kristin, and a couple of university buddies, but she didn't have any let-me-crash-on-your-living-room-floor-type friends.

Her mother lived in Melbourne, but they rarely communicated, which both saddened and appeased her. How strange to love someone in whose company you felt, more times than not, invisible. Once she would've performed somersaults to get her mother's attention. Later it seemed wiser to save her energy. Elaine Kendle had been stuck in a deep dark "if only" hole—probably was still stuck—and there was little Tamara could do about it.

Slapping his muscular thighs, Armand pushed to his feet. "I won't argue. If you want to stay 'til they come to evict you, which must be any day now, that's your choice."

He headed off and her mind froze. The walls that only a moment ago suffocated her, had receded until all she saw was Armand reaching for the tarnished knob. Opening the door. Walking away.

Her throat closed over.

"Wait!"

He pivoted back and their gazes fused. But she couldn't speak or move. Dammit, she wasn't used to accepting help.

From across the room, the light in his eyes changed from calculated disinterest to anticipation. In a measured gait, he returned and carefully reached out. She hesitated, then blew out a defeated breath and placed her hand in his.

As his fingers curled and swallowed hers, his warmth suffused her skin and swam up her arm, making every nerve ending skip and tingle. A smile lifted one side of the mouth. A masculine, sexy, wonder-how-it-feels mouth.

"Tell me what you need to take," he said, helping her up.

She nodded and together they collected a few things—some clothes, her books, and Einstein, her plant. But their movements, her situation, this handsome, insistent man…it all seemed surreal.

When the door clicked shut fifteen minutes later, she was still in a daze. Once more, her life had taken an acute, unexpected turn. She studied Armand, strong arms full of her "stuff" as he negotiated the stairwell, and wondered which of her barriers he'd attempt to break down next.

A big, baggy, chocolate-brown gaze, and breath that would bring water to a garlic clove's eye greeted Tamara.

Kneeling in Armand De Luca's enormous kitchen, she mentally blocked her nose and ruffled the sleepy bloodhound's ears with her good hand. "How long have you had Master? Since the last ice age?"

One hip propped against the island bench, shoulders set at an angle, Armand concentrated as he shuffled through mail he'd swept off the black granite counter. His gaze flicked up and he grinned a lopsided smile that made her stomach muscles flutter.

"Don't know about ice age," he said, attention return-ing to the mail. "Maybe around the time I started wearing long trousers."

Tamara's eye line slid down. "Long" by no means covered it. Nice in trousers, but delicious in the low-riding indigo-rinse jeans he'd changed into soon after they'd arrived home. And home, for the time being, was a magnificent Mediterranean-style residence in Sydney's most exclusive neighborhood.

Visible through an adjacent floor-to-ceiling window, towering pines decorated vast stretches of emerald-green lawn—foreground to a priceless harbor view, complete with colorful yachts and distant opera house shells. Inside, marble floors, stone columns, ornate sky-lights…the very air proclaimed unsurpassed extrava-gance and echoing space.

"This place is so big," she murmured. And quiet. She ruffled the dog's ears again. "I wonder if Master gets lonely."

There was no doubt that Armand spent most of his time at the office, and anyone could get lonesome, even a dog.

When Armand dropped the letters and moved toward her, Tamara held her bandaged wrist and reminded herself to breathe. His gait was predatory, but also languid, like a panther who wasn't the least concerned its kill would get away.

"The groundsman and Master have been friends for years. And he loves my housekeeper. You'll grow to love Ruth, too."

She'd met Ruth Sherman earlier and she did seem

nice. But Tamara didn't plan on developing a relationship. She pushed to her feet. "I won't be here that long."

He knotted powerful arms over an equally powerful chest. His hanging shirttails taunted her to come close and touch the washboard abs she felt sure lay beneath.

"So, you must have a plan."

Gaze snapping up, she focused. "Of course."

Crossing back to the gold-rimmed bench, he retrieved two steaming cups, one raspberry leaf tea (she carried a small supply in her handbag these days), one coffee freshly brewed in a contraption that probably cost more than a decent vacation. "Let me guess. Your plan is to find another job."

Her chin lifted. "Until recently, I've never been out of work."

"Not since leaving school at junior level."

His high-born barb pricked, but he'd seen the university textbooks. She was close to finishing a business degree, which, admittedly, had been a challenge, particularly her current unit of study; her second attempt at data analysis wasn't any easier than the first. Nevertheless she'd concede his point.

She moved to a meals table, which was tucked away in an all-glass bay window decorated with hanging baskets of lush maidenhair fern. "Yes, I did finish school early. And eventually went on to own my own company."

"Exemplar Events, an events coordination enterprise." Black glazed cups and saucers in hand, he joined her. "A hairdresser by trade, you found your true calling by accident after offering to organize events for friends and charity."

Forgetting to be annoyed at his detective work, she remembered back and smiled. "Christmas parties, school fetes, a couple of dinner fund-raisers." She had been so over mixing dyes and sweeping hair, and those events had been such fun.

"But the step up to corporate events was a steep one," he continued.

Full-scale pyrotechnics, first-class catering, together with clients' diverse special needs—each job had been exciting and she'd done well on her own…for a while. Ultimately, however, lack of business savvy had caught up. Figures weren't exactly her forte—not data analysis and not accounts receivable. When she ran aground, nothing could pull her free.

Armand slid the cups onto the table's sparkling glass surface. "A dissatisfied customer refused to pay for an extravagant function. The loss was too much on a shaky overdraft. The bank called in the loan. No other institution would bridge. You lost your business."

She gripped the back of a white wicker chair as regret and anger flooded her. "I lost everything." Thanks to Barclays Australasia.

Her five-year-old red coupe was the first to go. She'd loved that car. Then came the garage sales, the desperation. The repossession of her modest but dearly loved house would have been next, if the fire hadn't taken care of it first. Small print in the insurance policy translated into "goodbye, picket fence, hello tiny apartment." The deposit she'd sweated blood to save, all down the drain.

He pulled out her chair. "Life isn't always fair."

Though his words echoed her own thoughts, they sounded trite coming from Armand's privileged mouth. A millionaire couldn't possibly know the struggles small-business people faced to keep afloat.

She took her seat. Maybe he didn't deserve it, maybe he did. Either way, she couldn't help a dig. "Perhaps we should take another ride in your Bentley and you can tell me about what's fair."

His eyes glittered, with mischief or warning? "Retract the claws, Felix. I'm here to help, remember?"

More like help himself.

Armand's housekeeper breezed into the room, breaking their tension. Ruth defied all the rules associated with the term *housekeeper:* tall, svelte, smart civilian clothes rather than a drab uniform. In her early sixties, perhaps, she was still a striking woman: a salon-cut copper blonde with elegant sapphire starburst ear studs. The only giveaways to her vocation were an apron and brutally short nails. As Ruth laced her hands before her, hazel eyes half-mooning above a kind smile, Tamara wondered if she had grandchildren.

"Will there be anything else, sir?"

Armand's smile was fond. "I'll take care of everything from here on, thanks."

Ruth's comfortable gaze jumped to Tamara. "Good meeting you, Ms. Kendle."

Earlier the housekeeper had prepared a snack. With pregnancy hormones ambushing her appetite, ham and cheese on whole grain never tasted so good. "Thanks again for the sandwich, Ruth. It really hit the spot."

Headed for a corner of the kitchen, the older woman

brushed the compliment aside. "Wait 'til you taste my beef Wellington." She hung her apron on the back of the pantry door. "It's his favorite."

Sitting alongside Tamara now, Armand scooped a heap of sugar into his cup. "Your choc-mint cheesecake is my favorite."

Ruth mouthed to Tamara, "Sweet tooth," then said aloud, "I'll be in early tomorrow. Master needs to go to the vet—"

"I'll take care of that," Armand let her know, stirring. "Have a good weekend."

Ruth winked at Tamara and headed out the room. "See you Monday."

Shoulders sagging, Tamara gave in to a sigh. Guess she would at that.

While she gathered her cup close and filled her lungs with the sweet herbal aroma, Armand set their conversation back on track.

"We were discussing the death of your business."

A nasty shiver ran through her. Did he have to put it like that?

She set her cup down. "I might be in a tight place at the moment, but I'll get by." She always had.

His furrowed gaze challenged hers. "Like your mother got by?"

Her throat swelled, cutting off air. Despite the neglect, she loved her mother and wanted to include her in her baby's life. And if he dared mention her father…!

Some things were best left buried.

"My mother has nothing to do with this."

He weighed her statement before he cocked a brow

and drank. The cup landed back in its saucer with a clatter. "You're right. This is about you and what opportunities you, as a mother, decide to give or deny your child."

A knot twisted in her stomach. Money didn't guarantee happiness. Still, given her less than stellar start in life, Tamara knew full well food and clothes didn't materialize out of thin air. She leveled him a look. "That's not fair."

"I believe we've had that discussion."

So cool. So suave. So blasted infuriating!

She surged up from her chair.

By the window, she dragged a gaze around the outside view to where a bust of what looked like a satyr guarded a garden entrance. Orderly, pristine, clutter-free. Must cost a fortune to maintain.

Her days wouldn't shorten after the baby was born, particularly once she was ready to rebuild her business. On top of that, having no partner meant not only long hours on the job, but longer childcare hours, too.

The tip of her index finger trailed down the glass, then drew three times over a horizontal figure eight.

A marriage of convenience…to Armand De Luca… no more struggle…no more treading water.

A razor-sharp pang coiled inside of her. Her hand clenched and dropped.

What on earth was she thinking? She wanted to be in love with the man she married, not indebted. Surely that wasn't expecting too much, even with all the uncertainty clouding her life. Even given the way Armand made her feel…temporarily rescued.

Her stomach jumped when Armand's heat-infused

palm came to rest on her shoulder, but she dared not face him. The flare of his touch was enough to unhinge her. She wouldn't risk more confusion by looking into those eyes.

His breath warmed her crown as his voice rumbled at her ear. "Weigh your options carefully. Consider the opportunities you'd give your child, now and in the future."

A future with opportunities, security, a name that opened doors. And all she had to do was marry a stranger.

She chewed her lip and struggled to form the question that had scratched at her mind since this man, more like a phantom, had swept into her life.

"Don't get the idea I'm saying yes, because I'm not, but…" Her mouth was cracker-dry. She fought to swallow against the choking beat of her heart vibrating up her throat. "If we were to wed, if we were to become man and wife…"

A hot flush washed through her. She couldn't say the words.

"Would the marriage include conjugal rights?"

As his question soaked in, cool dots of perspiration broke along her hairline. From the corner of her eye she saw his long blunt fingers splayed over the shoulder of her white cotton shirt, the glint of his dress ring's ruby catching the last of the day's old-gold light. Suddenly she couldn't get enough air. Couldn't stop the mad thudding in her chest.

Shoulder dipping, she edged away. His hand withdrew. Good. Some space. She couldn't think straight otherwise.

She filled her lungs with oxygen and courage.

Conjugal rights. She cringed. "That's such an old-fashioned term."

"Marriage is an old-fashioned and serious institution." Though he didn't touch her again, she felt the vacuum of his natural heat to her core, the somber conviction of his words. "Creating, and maintaining, physical bonds are an important part of a relationship."

"Physical." A typical male response. "What about emotional bonds?"

"Can you think of a better way to feel close to someone than sexual intimacy? If you agree to marry me, Tamara, you agree to share my bed, and no one else's."

"You make it sound like a command."

But the sparks firing over her skin weren't entirely from indignation. Part of her shrank from the idea of sleeping with a man she barely knew. Another more secret part wondered at the idea of sampling his kisses, coming to know the rasp of his end-of-day beard as he held her, exploring, coaxing. If it was wrong to think that way, if it was somehow disrespectful to Marc's memory, God help her, she couldn't help it. Not with Armand so close, speaking about his bed and marriage and sex.

As if reading her mind, he nudged closer. Her back to him, she felt his hot gaze climb her bare arm, leaving a fog of steam in its wake.

"The idea of consummating our marriage worries you?"

As his deep voice strummed through her blood like a chord of bass music, an image of his mouth claiming hers came to mind, a vision of his strong naked body pinning her own. A drugging heat seeped through her tummy and her eyes drifted closed.

This was too intense. Too soon.

She turned a tight circle to face him—or, rather, the wall of his chest and the subtle tease in his gaze. Steeling herself, she shouldered past him, back toward the table. "You're dealing with a woman who believes in fairy tales. Don't get ahead of yourself, Mr. De Luca."

"Armand, remember?"

A slanted grin enhanced the seductive line of his mouth. Palm pressed against her jumping stomach, she pried her gaze away. They'd talked enough.

She headed for a twelve-foot-high archway that led to a sweeping staircase and, eventually, the privacy of the suite she'd been shown earlier. "I was on the phone when you arrived at my apartment. If I can use the extension in my room, I'd like to call her back."

"A friend?"

"Melanie Harris. Marc's friend, too."

"Does she know about the baby?"

Tamara's heart contracted and her pace faltered. She'd told no one but Marc. In fact, the only two people in the world who knew were in this room. "No one knows about that night but you," she said over her shoulder.

"Good."

She frowned. Maybe she hadn't heard him right. She stopped and inched around. His eyes looked incredibly dark, as if something lurked beneath. A tremor of unease rippled through her system. "What do you mean, 'good'?"

Slotting hands in his back jeans pockets, he seemed to choose his words. "The will stipulates a legitimate heir."

She took a moment to digest his deeper meaning. "You want people to believe this baby is…" She hunted for a clinical phrase. "Biologically yours and mine?"

"The law views any child born after marriage as legitimate…unless paternity is challenged. No one knowing simply makes it more—" he hesitated again "—convenient."

He spoke as if the issue of paternity held no emotional worth. "You don't want anyone to know about the true father to make doubly sure the terms of a will are met?"

She could never do that to Marc, and this child certainly deserved to know the name of his father. Tamara only wished she'd been given that courtesy.

Armand's eyes flashed before his hands withdrew from his pockets and he moved closer. "To the contrary. It's only respectful to acknowledge your roots, no matter the circumstances. When the child is old enough, everything will be settled and he will know his origins."

The double knot in her chest released a bit. Breathing again, she nodded and they walked together beneath the arch. For Armand to gain control of his empire, De Luca Senior had stipulated he produce a legitimate heir. The solution seemed obvious.

"Can't a nephew or niece be a legitimate heir? What about an adopted child?"

"Not under the terms of this will. The clause is specific." Armand's concerned gaze skimmed her face. "We'll talk more tomorrow. You look tired."

Not tired, she realized anew. Utterly drained. Her legs felt like lead logs. "It would be good to lie down," she conceded, aware of his hand on the small of her back as he steered her through an adjoining sitting area where a portrait of a stern-looking man presided over a limestone chimneypiece.

"Wrist hurting?"

Hauling her gaze away from the picture's flint-hard dark eyes, she shucked off a shiver. "It's fine."

"I'm not sure I did a good enough job on that bandage. I'll take you to a doctor tomorrow. And not just for your wrist."

"The bandage is fine." He'd taken great care to wind it neither too loose nor too tight. "And if you're referring to the baby, I'll see my own doctor." A general practitioner, not a specialist, whom Tamara felt comfortable with and trusted. An OB would come later.

"We'll discuss it tomorrow." His tone indicated his mind was made up.

Surprisingly, curiosity overrode irritation. "Are you always this bossy?"

His face remained deadpan. "Occupational hazard." They reached the stairs and ascended in step. "After the doctor, we'll head in to town and choose wedding invitations."

A chorus of alarm bells blared in her head. She hadn't agreed to anything yet! She pitched him a distressed glance.

Those devilish blue eyes were grinning. "I like to be prepared."

CHAPTER THREE

IN De Luca Enterprises' inner-city penthouse office, Armand eased up from his high-backed chair, a smile spread clean across his face. Knee deep in figures from his trip to Beijing last week, his secretary knew he shouldn't be disturbed. However, there were always exceptions to the rule.

Rounding the massive desk, he extended his hand in welcome as one side of the double oak doors fanned back and a man Armand had known all his life strode in. "Matthew, I wondered if you'd decided against returning from vacation altogether."

Tall and lean, Matthew could have been ten years younger than his sixty-five. He chuckled. "You know how I love this company, but these past six weeks made me realize three years is too long to wait for a break. You haven't lived 'til you enjoy old-style Hawaii and Hamoa Beach. Total relaxation."

He looked tanned and healthy. But the difference went beyond that. When Armand released Matthew's right hand, he found the answer shining on his left. A gold band. Disbelief fell through him, then a startled laugh coughed out. "My God, you're married!"

Looking like the old tomcat who'd eaten the last of the cream, Matthew moved toward the maroon chesterfield. "We met at a legal colleague's retirement party three months ago." A far-off, contented gleam softened ice-blue eyes as he folded into the settee and flicked open his jacket buttons. "I thought I was well over such foolishness. Evie changed all that."

Shock didn't begin to describe the emotion, but if Matthew was happy, Armand was happy for him. Clapping his hands and rubbing, he set off for the wet bar. "This calls for a toast."

When Armand returned with two glasses, they saluted and drank. "Vintage Macallan?"

"A special malt for a special occasion."

Matthew focused on the younger man then slowly shook his head. "Never once did I dream I'd beat you to the altar."

"You were a confirmed bachelor. She must be special."

Swirling his glass, Matthew raised his brows and sighed. "She is at that." He studied the liquor's oak-tint color for a long moment. "No new love interest on your horizon, I suppose."

Regularly since his father's death, Matthew had tentatively asked about prospective fiancées, after which he would mention the will then, just as predictably, assure Armand not to worry. The balance of the trust was in good hands...*his* hands. He was an experienced lawyer, loyal board member and devoted family friend. No matter if the heir came a little late, Matthew would ensure

Armand got what he deserved. If all went according to plan, today would be the final time Matthew need ask.

Confident, Armand replied, "Actually, I intend to announce my own wedding date very soon." Despite his friend's assurance about the trust, he wanted to get the matrimonial legalities cleared up.

Matthew's expression sagged in astonishment and his face blanched. A hand funneled through his high silver-gray hairline as he released a laugh. "Well, do I know the lucky girl?"

Armand swallowed his scotch and grunted in the negative. "She's not society."

"From humble beginnings then?"

Armand nodded.

"Like your mother."

Fingers of tension circled Armand's throat. He swallowed past the sensation and turned to his desk. He didn't need the comparison. Six years ago he'd asked for the hand of a woman who hailed from an impeccable family line, and look how that turned out. Christine Sawyer had tried to hock the ring—a family heirloom, for Pete's sake. So much for blue-blood pedigree. So much for true love.

Matthew's apologetic voice followed him. "Forgive me. That was unnecessary. I'm sure she'll fit in beautifully. What's her name?"

Armand set down his glass and drew in his chair. "Tamara Kendle."

Matthew nodded, sipped, smiled. "Eager to start a family, no doubt."

"You could say that."

Throughout the week, Tamara's bouts of morning sickness had left her wan, but by evening her face glowed. Not that she would admit her favorable adjustment anytime soon. She was, indeed, a minx, constantly challenging him with her jibes and bold green eyes. But last night she hadn't mentioned leaving once. *Progress.* Tonight he planned to push that advantage as far as it would go.

Armand's attention landed on the file he'd been working on and his mind clicked over. He caught the time on his watch. After five. Matthew would want to return to his bride, but a quick nod here first would be appreciated.

Armand rapped the file. "Do you have a minute?"

Matthew unraveled his legs. "China?" His expression filled with interest, as he moved to stand beside Armand's chair.

Armand opened the file and flipped through. "The consultant had it right. At least two areas would fit our needs exactly." He indicated a map, pointing out Shanghai and Hang Zhou. "Of course we'd still keep our plants in Australia, but increase output by expanding and make a decent profit, even factoring in shipping. The businessmen I spoke with over there are keen."

Armand leaned back, hands laced behind his head. Innovative growth strategies and organizing new trade links not only kept him alert, but such measures were also vital. Building upon De Luca Enterprises' place in today's competitive manufacturing and corporate world meant breathing a constant stream of fresh air into the business. Without new initiatives, DLE could stagnate, stumble, or worse, risk takeover. He didn't advocate violence, but he'd sooner fight to the death than hand over his heart and soul to any man.

Concentrating on the file, Armand tipped forward again. "I still estimate we need to shift between eighteen and twenty percent of primary holdings to fund establishment costs."

He waited while Matthew perused the figures, absently correcting the knot in the tie Armand hadn't seen before; a frugal man of habit, Matthew had worn either the crimson, the green or the striped gray for countless years. Armand grinned. The little woman must be making changes.

Matthew closed the folder, then tucked it under an arm. "Let me take this and go through the negotiation side. You need to be sensitive when dealing with other cultures. Don't want to get anyone offside by coming across as ignorant," he said, chuckling, "or arrogant."

Appreciating the advice, Armand smiled and nodded. "The groundwork's complete. I'd like to move forward and propose this ASAP, before the half-year profit report and dividend announcement is released."

The interim report had indicated a healthy profit, but final figures wouldn't be available for, perhaps, three months. He didn't want to give the conservative element of the board a chance to fixate upon concrete profit margins, then veto his expansion plans as unnecessary or risky. Armand preferred to see his plans as discerning.

For some odd reason, Armand felt a niggling doubt but quickly pushed the frown away. This man was loyal.

There was no reason to believe Matthew wouldn't stand by him now.

When Matthew moved away and Armand stood to show him out, his thoughts reverted to the earlier news. "We four must do dinner soon." Once everything was set with Tamara.

Matthew clapped his protégé on the back. "I'll let Evie know."

Half an hour later, Armand was home. Loosening his tie and releasing his collar button, he called out a hello, then strode from room to room. Ruth had the afternoon off. She now knew about the situation between himself and Tamara, and that tonight he planned to take their guest to a new restaurant with superb, glittering night views and the best chocolate mousse truffles in all of Sydney. But Master was MIA, too. And where was Tamara?

A brainwave struck and he marched into her favorite room in the house. He scouted around the library, even angling a look upward over the vast shelves that reached to the vaulted, paneled ceiling. Tamara said she loved the smell of so many books.

Jaw clenched, he strode out.

She wouldn't have left without a word. She knew he'd only track her down. Besides, as this week had unfolded, her resistance had lessened. He noticed her leanings in subtle ways, like her growing practice to sit with him in the evenings. Long legs tucked under, she would read a fat novel or her study book while he went over figures or proposals in his wing chair, Master sprawled out near the footstool.

He noticed an increase and variety in Tamara's conversations, too, not simply about their situation, but more commonplace interests—current affairs, music, movies. Romantic comedies weren't his speed, but he'd enjoyed listening to her laugh when they'd watched a recent release.

He also enjoyed the way her body looked draped over the chintz couch…smooth cinnamon-tinted skin, long hair, shiny as black satin. When she lost herself in a chapter, her full lips would part and her breasts would rise and fall a little faster with her breathing. She'd twine a length of hair with her index finger, 'round and 'round 'til he wanted to leap over and grab her hand, then coax her mouth still wider using solely the persuasion of his own.

Hands low on hips, he cast a blank look around that lounge room now. Where the hell was she?

Then it dawned.

He found her swimming laps in the indoor pool's sparkling blue length, wrist obviously mended, barely a ripple in her wake. Her flawless movements, that stream of hair…everything about her exuded grace, precision. Beauty.

His groin and heart throbbed in tandem.

Sexual attraction was one thing; they had that going for them in spades and very soon he'd have her admit it. But this emotional tug?

Armand butted his shoulder against the twenty-foot jamb, clenching then flexing a hand.

Clearly his connection to this woman was based on the baby she carried. Marco could choose to ignore the family name and legacy, even after barriers had been erased. But Marco's child would be raised knowing he was a De Luca. As Tamara had so wisely pointed out, family was important, more important than anything—and now nothing stood in the way of cementing that moral foundation and putting words into practice. The long-ago wrong would finally be righted.

Rounding off a lap, Tamara jettisoned out of the middle lane onto the expansive terracotta tiles. One knee bent up, the other dangled in the water—sweeping languidly back and forth—she wrung her heavy mane then shook it out. Droplets flew, darkening the tiles in a splatter of dots.

Aware of his elevated heartbeat and perspiration forming along his brow, Armand could only gaze at long slim limbs and high firm breasts that talked to him of sin and more sin. But her hair beguiled him most, spilling over her shoulders. Shoulders he would knead when he pressed her into silk sheets on their wedding night.

Much sooner than that, if he had anything to do with it.

Wide eyes centered on his. She pushed to her feet then, with two hands, smoothed back tangles of hair that had fallen over her face. Her throat bobbed as she swallowed her surprise. "I didn't expect you home so soon."

"My last meeting was cancelled." No need to tell her he'd been the one to defer.

She lowered her arms. "And there wasn't a single thing to keep you occupied? I'd pegged you for a workaholic."

He found a plaintive tone. "It is Friday."

Her lips curved into a teasing smile. "Well, I suppose, in that case…"

She ran a speculative eye all the way down to his shoes before catching herself and moving in a purposeful step to a nearby deckchair. When she flicked a large white towel from its back and patted each arm, both anticipation and regret hummed through his veins. He didn't want her dry. He wanted that red one-piece plied against him, wet, warm and salaciously wanting. Today that seemed more likely than ever.

He hadn't imagined her mounting curiosity, the inquisitive looks ventured beneath lowered lashes, the way the air steamed and thickened whenever they were close enough to touch. She still grieved for Marco, but as a friend; the fairy-tale feelings she yearned for weren't involved.

He couldn't give her the fantasy, either; that part of him was buried forever. However, if she wanted the illusion of love so badly, if she wanted to believe their future would be built on violin chords and bow-strung cupids, what harm was there? In fact, it could work in his favor.

Sauntering over, he released one gold cufflink, then the other, and weighed them in a palm. "Have you made a decision regarding my proposal? You've been here a week."

She visibly paled before spilling out a laugh. "Right. One whole week."

"You understand the time restraints."

Unmoved, she dabbed her throat. "Your birthday's months away."

"Arrangements need to be made."

Towel cupping one side of her face, she stopped to stare as if he'd spouted horns. "This isn't a small decision."

He dropped the links into his top pocket. "It's a huge decision, but the right one for your child. For you, too, Tamara."

She quarter-turned from him, not listening. A number of adjectives besides *headstrong* sprang to his mind. Best try a different tack.

Hands slotting into his trousers' pockets, he moved closer. "How's the assignment going?"

Leaning over to towel one gorgeous calf, she faltered. "It's…coming along."

"If you want help, figures are my second language." Not that she'd need that degree when they were married.

She lashed the enormous towel under her arms, sari-style. All that remained of that sensational view were ankles and red-tipped toes.

Time to pull out the big guns.

Stopping inches away, he peered down, willing her to bend and submit to the inevitable. He wouldn't give up. Quitting wasn't in his makeup, and if she lost the bravado, she could admit she wanted him, too.

Heat spread in his chest and his expression purposely softened at the same time their smoldering connection strengthened and swelled. He spoke to her lips. "Say you're considering it."

Hitching up the towel, she gave him a shaky, glassy-eyed smile. "I'm fine with the assignment, truly."

"Not the assignment." His hands came out of his pockets. "My proposal."

They shared a meaningful look, her darkening eyes betraying more than she might like. She abruptly averted her gaze, pushing more hair from her face. "Can we talk about this later?"

Not a chance.

"Say it."

Her hunted gaze snapped up. She shook her head, bit her lip. Good God, that swimsuit had looked fine. How his fingers burned to reach out and touch.

Finally, after a torturous moment, she gave in to a halfhearted growl and a shrug. "Oh, hell. All right. Yes, I'm considering it."

Again his attention strayed to her lips, dusky pink, naturally full, meant to be kissed, and kissed often.

He lifted one brow. "Anything I can do to tip the scales?"

A droplet trailed from the gold cross to her cleavage as she inhaled deeply. "Giving me a place to stay and stocking me with a wardrobe Hollywood starlets would envy is plenty for now."

After seeing her couple of inexpensive outfits, he'd put his assistant on the case. Twenty-four hours later, a leading fashion consultant had delivered a range of outfits to his door. The sizing, styles and color choices had been perfect. By the third day, Tamara had given up protesting.

"You'll need another gown soon," he told her in a low, compelling voice. "A wedding gown."

While he imagined her in a stunning white sheath and streaming veil, she stumbled back. "Wait a minute. I haven't decided anything yet."

That higher impulse, reshaping and growing each day, saw its chance. "Then let me help."

A single arm wound out and he swept her close. Eyes bulging saucer-wide, she gasped as their bridged kindling leapt into flame. Relishing her damp frame against his body, he hushed her parted lips with the pad of his thumb a heartbeat before his mouth came down.

She bucked. Wedged between them, her small fists squirmed against his shirtfront. But, with one large hand cupping her rump and the other bracing her head, he held her mouth on his. He knew what he was doing. Just a second or two more…

He deepened the kiss 'til her already weakened chains fell and her natural scent and budding desire mingled to surround and invite him in. Finally she melted, her fingers spreading to knead rather than push at the sinew beneath his shirt.

When she sighed soft and deep in her throat, his every participating cell upped a gear, from pleasurable tactic to ready fascination. Raw heat snaked through his bloodstream, lava edging over stone, warming the back of his knees, leaving pinpoints of fire where her finger pads pressed.

He shifted, his right hand threaded through the silky underbrush of her hair. He massaged her nape and she melted more.

After an endless moment, they slowly parted, mouths soft and moist. The surroundings seeped into his consciousness, but while his eyes reluctantly opened, hers remained closed. As physical longing fermented and bubbled up through his layers, Armand smiled.

This could work out nicely.

His fingers trailed down the sweep of flesh that

joined her throat to her shoulder. He squeezed gently and she trembled. "Tamara."

Her dreamy eyes flickered open. Fond recognition instantly shuttered behind a vulnerability that made his throat grow thick even as the embers in the pit of his stomach smoldered bright red.

Her mouth pressed together. She looked so torn. "I'm still thinking."

"Perhaps you're making the decision harder than it needs to be." The residue of smoky passion evaporated from her eyes and she wrenched to be free, but he overlooked her wavering and declined to release her. Their gazes fixed again, hers fierce, his placating yet assured.

"I'm not the enemy, Tamara." His earlier thought resurfaced and he veered down another path. "All the best fairy tales begin with conflict. Look at *Beauty and the Beast.*"

She didn't buy it. "You don't believe in fairy tales."

"Maybe I just need that special someone to help me believe."

He pushed aside a twinge at such shameless deceit and focused on the future, on her changed expression—wondering, hopeful. When his fingertip feathered down her temple around her chin, she shivered but didn't jerk away. He ought to kiss her again; she wouldn't resist. But the most successful seductions used a number of devices, including the guarantee of time. It meant delaying gratification, but even the brightest day eventually surrendered to the night.

His hand sluiced down her arm before he edged away. Her posture slumped the barest amount as if, despite her grit, she'd relied on the support. He hid his satisfaction behind a quiet smile.

"We're going out tonight," he announced, turning on his heel. "Wear something elegant." No need to suggest she leave her hair down. Thankfully she usually did.

Her response was evasive. "I'm a little tired."

He found his tie's longest end and tugged it from his collar in one fluid deliberate action. "We can always stay in."

Her shoulders came up as she hugged the towel close. "That's okay. I'm sure I'll be fine."

"Let's say seven then. Can't speak for you—" his gaze licked her body "—but I'm starving."

CHAPTER FOUR

TAMARA didn't like surprises. She preferred to see what was ahead and strategize well in advance the best course of action. "Whirlwind adventure" was not on her must-do list. Then Armand De Luca had exploded into her life.

These past few days Armand had treated her like a princess, taking her out to dinner, engaging her in stimulating conversation, finding opportunities to touch her—a stroke of her cheek, a casual arm threaded around her waist. Last night, as they'd slow danced together after a delicious meal at one of Sydney's top venues, he'd stolen another kiss. While her mind had resisted, her body had cried out for more.

This December morning when he'd suggested an impromptu outing to Sydney's largest mall, Tamara had been cautious. The gleam in his eye told her he had something planned. Now, as he cleaved a path for them through the congested slab of shoppers, she wondered if those plans included jewelry stores and diamond rings.

He glanced over and took her hand. His smile, a

dazzling combination of ease and charm, sent her stomach into immediate freefall. The sensation must have shown on her face.

His smile faded. "You need to rest."

He constantly worried for her health, which was amusing, or touching, more so than annoying. "I feel great."

No morning sickness and for the first time in ages she was energetic and cheerful, a far cry from her condition a month ago when her life had felt tossed upside down in a trash can. These last two weeks living under Armand's roof had made all the difference and she couldn't help but be grateful. Just as she couldn't help feeling lured by his unique brand of laid-back charm, or the palpable strength of their simmering physical attraction.

His kiss last night had left her troubled, shaky, but ultimately anticipating the next. After sharing time together and discovering a little of the man behind the name, Tamara's feelings had shifted considerably.

She'd begun to care.

Maybe it was pregnancy hormones prompting her to attach, but she wasn't wholly surprised by her swing in emotions. She'd like to see any woman resist Armand's heavy-lidded eyes and dominating presence, which so effortlessly commanded attention and admiration wherever he went. However, while her heart whispered, Accept, believe, say yes, her head still waved a red flag.

Armand De Luca was a tactician, an astute business-man. He needed to seal an important transaction and he needed her to do it. Just because she'd begun to care for him didn't make it reciprocal. His mention of fairy tales, that kiss last night, the softer looks…surely they were all means to an end. She didn't want to fool herself into believing it was anything else. She didn't like surprises, but she disliked disappointment more.

He glanced at his platinum watch then shucked back one shoulder. The canary-yellow of his jersey-knit shirt was a beacon against his muscular bronzed arms and tanned vee at his neck. Her gaze traveled higher and her heartbeat stuttered at the sight of his frown.

"Is something wrong?"

His attention shot from the crowds back to her and the wattage on his smile tweaked up again. "Just running over the agenda for this afternoon's meeting."

She groaned. "But it's Saturday."

Before the words were out she wanted to swallow them. Men like Armand lived to work, not the other way around. She'd always admired a strong work ethic, yet today she couldn't help but wish he didn't have to rush off. He'd worked late night before last. She'd waited 'til eleven before taking herself off to her cloud of a bed. Master had looked abandoned, so he'd come, too.

In the heart of the mall, they skirted around a towering fir dressed in giant silver bells and scarlet gold-trimmed bows while Bing Crosby crooned "I'll be Home for Christmas" through the speakers.

"I organized a board meeting," Armand said. "At short notice, this was the best fit day for everyone."

"What's so urgent?"

Weird. A couple of months ago, Tamara would have scowled at such a question; everything associated with her own company had seemed so urgent. Yet, although she was determined to some day regenerate her business, her Exemplar Events days now seemed strangely distant, as if they existed at some far-off point she viewed through a telescope.

Which, to a lesser degree, also reflected her feelings regarding Marc. Her friend would never be forgotten, but the sharpest edge of her pain had dulled. Sometimes she managed a smile instead of tearing up when she thought of him. From the sound of their more general phone calls, it seemed Melanie and Kristin had begun to accept the inevitable, too. Which was what Marc would have wanted them to do…think of him fondly and move on with their lives.

Thick garlands of gold, emerald and red glittered above as she and Armand crossed an entrance into a big-name department store. He ushered her down an aisle parading regiments of stainless steel appliances.

"The meeting's about my proposal for overseas expansion. We spoke about it the other night."

She remembered. His eyes had gleamed like blue marbles when he'd explained how he, as CEO, needed to continually strategize to keep De Luca Enterprises on a top rung in the global picture. Sometimes she wondered how he managed to spend any time at home. What would that mean when the baby arrived?

Of course, his office hours really only mattered if she decided to accept his offer of marriage. She still hadn't made up her mind. Not completely.

"I don't expect any hassles this afternoon," he said as they dropped pace to appreciate Santa's gingerbread house and a line of rapt children waiting for a private audience. "I need a motion passed, then everyone can be on their way."

"Will Matthew Mohill be there?" The name had stuck. Dante's friend, the man Armand's father had entrusted with the balance of interest in the company.

Armand nodded. "Matthew's a respected member of the board. He knows the company inside out, plus he's my most loyal supporter. He could vote by proxy, but I wouldn't think of conducting a meeting like this without him."

But something in his expression made Tamara wonder if Armand was so sure.

He stopped to jerk his chin at Santa, ho-ho-ing from a giant red chair lined with faux-fur trim. "While we're here, you want to put in a request to the bearded gent?"

She sighed. "This might sound cheesy, but the only thing I truly want is a healthy baby."

Her hand still in his, he turned to face her, his eyes brimming with a profound interest she'd come to recognize and secretly long for.

"Then I'll make a wish," he said.

She teased, "Have you been a good boy?"

"Painfully good."

When he looked at her like that, as if she were a spoonful of his favorite dessert, it was hard to think straight let alone carry on a conversation.

She nodded. "All right. But since you're old enough to sleep without a night-light, you're eligible for only one wish."

He tightened his clasp and pressed the back of her hand against his belt. "I wish I didn't have to be good anymore."

The delicious glow at her center spread to devour her limbs. Her heartbeat banged at the top of her throat and she could barely push her voice past the swell. "Santa wouldn't be pleased to hear that."

"He's not the one who counts."

She trembled, certain he would take the next step, thatch his fingers up through the back of her hair and steal the kiss she couldn't help but ache to give.

"You should be careful," she murmured. "Santa's helpers are everywhere."

He analyzed every nuance of her face while he slid her hand up the steel struts of his stomach and higher, over the hot groove of his chest. "Here's something else. I won't be satisfied with only one wish."

Muscles gone to jelly, she leaned against the pylon at her back. "And if you had to stop at one?"

"I'd rather be greedy."

"There's a saying," she told him. "Perhaps your eyes are too big."

He grinned. "Oh, not my eyes."

Deep inside, raked coals began to smolder. Bing and the shoppers faded into nonexistence as his other arm raised to brace his weight above her head. He tipped so close she could already taste him.

She swallowed involuntarily. "I don't think we're talking about Christmas wishes anymore."

"Me, either. Christmas is a week away."

He didn't seem the least concerned they were in a public place—that people were stopping to smile and titter. Tamara knew that in another time with anyone else she would be embarrassed, but with Armand, it was difficult to decipher between what was proper and what was not. She only knew the pleasure of being this near to his strength and his will outweighed by far any guilt.

His raised bicep flexed as his mouth came close to brush her hair. "Do you think we should keep shopping or work up more of a crowd?"

She shivered all the way to her toes. "I think you don't know how to spell the word *good*."

"But you're wrong. It starts with *Y* and ends with you."

He nipped her ear and tiny quills quivered deep inside. If he hadn't shown some mercy, she might have slid in a puddle to the floor. Instead, looking pleased with her response, he rocked back and turned to start off again.

She had to grin. He wasn't good, he was exceptional.

Her breathing had returned to normal by the time they stopped before a series of drawn velvet curtains that seemed to be awaiting them. The band of his arm urged her closer and she melded against the masculine pillar of his frame. In her heart of hearts, she didn't want to fight their attraction, and by now she was afraid he was fully aware of it.

A well-groomed store employee appeared, her pretty face split with a smitten puppy-dog smile. "Mr. De Luca, we have everything ready, just as you requested."

Tamara sent him an assessing look. "I knew you had something planned."

His crooked smile burrowed in to warm her all over again. "Just a little surprise."

Lost for ideas, she hitched a shoulder and let it drop. "What?"

Obviously not engagement rings, and hopefully not

more clothes. She already chose from scores of designer labels hanging in her giant walk-in closet, including today's tangerine-colored summer dress. She felt like a princess in its light-as-gossamer flowing skirt. Then again she'd feel like a princess in a cotton sack with this man as her escort.

Attention fixed on the crimson curtains, Armand eased them both forward. "If nothing suits, just say."

Tamara's nerve endings jangled. The little girl inside her was dying to discover what lay beyond, but the cautious woman wasn't sure she wanted to know. Anxiety won and the words tumbled out. "I don't like surprises."

He peered across, his expression intense yet comforting. "You'll like this one."

As if by royal command, the curtains magically opened and Tamara's heart leapt, then thumped like a bongo drum. Too late she clasped a hand over her mouth to catch a small cry of delight.

Behind each curtain was a nursery display, a beautiful baby's room. The first was in exquisite, highly polished rosewood. The second was a fantasy in lacquered white and fine netting. The third had well-known cartoon characters leaping off the walls, rugs and blankets. The fourth was yesteryear, tranquil mauve satin and cream lace. Fifth in line was brilliantly contemporary, vivid pinks and iridescent blues. Oh, but the sixth…

Her enchanted gaze slid over the *broderie anglaise* bumper and quilt set, the enormous A-frame dollhouse in one corner and vintage train set chugging away in another. She saw her newborn swaddled in the white cane crib and even heard the lullaby she would sing as she nursed in the rocking chair.

She blinked through her misted vision. "This is…"

"Too much?"

"No. Perfect!"

Fists settling low on his hips, Armand studied the scene and nodded. "I think so, too. Perfect."

Tugged along by the invisible string that linked her to this final display, Tamara crossed toward the cot, Armand in step at her side. She stroked the beautifully embroidered fabric then bit her lip at a jab of doubt.

But even a ruthless steel magnate wouldn't manipulate a woman's emotions to this extent solely to achieve his aim. She stole a glance at his profile—straight nose, invincible jaw, satisfaction radiating from his every pore. No one was that good an actor. Were they?

He'd said more than once he wanted to provide the baby with two parents, a sound family life. Surely any loving mother would want the same. Armand had insinuated he might even be swayed into basing a marriage on more than practicality.

Maybe I just need that special someone to help me believe.

If only she could be sure he was sincere.

His twinkling gaze met hers and Tamara's pulse rate spiked. At times he could be too forceful, more than a touch arrogant, but right now he seemed too good to be true.

"Are you sure you're happy with everything." He tossed another a look around. "Maybe you'd like something extra."

The young woman shuffled forward, hands clasped before her. "We have gorgeous teddy bears, up to ten feet tall."

Gaze caressing, Armand shifted around to stand in front of her. "The lady said she has bears."

Tamara's eyes closed briefly against the drug of his innate heat and the image of sand running through an hourglass. She had a decision to make. And there was no turning back now.

An hour later, with the soft top down on Armand's classic E-type Jaguar, they raced along a winding ocean road. Tamara didn't dare glance at the speedometer, but rather clung to the tan leather armrest, binding in the other hand her streaming hair.

Armand's eyes were hidden beneath mirror sunglasses. His widow's peak flashed in and out of view as he changed gears, wind tunneling through his inky hair. Only his set jaw and the hint of a grin bespoke of his unbridled love of speed.

They traveled too fast to allow conversation, not that Tamara minded. She was enjoying herself as she'd never done before. What a new and exhilarating form of release. Pedal to the metal, inhibitions cast to the wind and an attractive, wealthy suitor at her side. The heady thrill was almost enough to make her forget the extraordinary situation that had thrown them together.

The Jag veered off behind a blanket of pine trees and came to standstill at the edge of a precipice. Tamara lost her breath at the spectacular view. The

Pacific Ocean seemed endless and, at this distance, somehow motionless yet surging with unleashed energy and life. A crisp briny wind caught her hair, whipping it against her cheeks. The experience of solitude, of strangely owning the world from this unreachable point, was surreal.

Armand pulled the car off the road. He helped her out then retrieved a red-checked blanket from the boot. He stretched it over a concave curve of grass then, one finger curling, beckoned her near. "Sit with me."

Tellingly warm, she inhaled the pine and sea air then inched forward. "We're miles from anywhere." She risked a gibe that wasn't all tease. "Can I trust you?"

He flipped the glasses back on his head. "You're worried I'll throw you over the cliff—" his smile was killer-sexy "—or down on the ground?"

Oxygen evaporated in her lungs as flash fires ignited over her body. Biting her inside cheek, she braced herself against the barrage of giddy sensation. What did he have in store?

Fighting the urge to pat down her burning cheeks, she held the flapping spread of her skirt, kicked off her heels and lowered down onto the blanket. They sat in a slight hollow, the fresh wind blowing over their heads.

Armand laid full-length, his weight propped upon one elbow. He grasped a seed-blown dandelion from a nearby clutch and twirled it, back and forth, between finger and thumb. That ruby ring glinted in the midday sun as he held the dried flower high. Gusts peeled the fluffy spikes from its stem and spirited them away like tiny angels flying home.

He focused on the blue expanse. "I love the sea. The enormity. The solitude." He tossed the dandelion stick to the wind. "We should take my boat out soon."

Smoothing the blanket beside her, she grinned. "Boat or ship?"

"A fifty-foot yacht," he said, matter-of-factly. "I usually upgrade each year or so. But this one…" He peered off into the waves. "Well, she's something special. My first craft was a skull. I'd go out with friends and we'd burn our muscles rowing her for hours."

"Sounds like torture." She leant back on her hands. "But I guess it's no different to the endorphin buzz I get swimming laps."

The same kind of control, yet release. In her early teens she'd visit the local public pool and freestyle 'til her limbs felt ready to fall off, but the logic was simple. The longer she'd spent there chewing up excess energy, the less time she had to sit at home alone.

Tamara tilted her face toward the sun's warm rays. "You still row with your friends?"

"Not so much now, but we keep in touch. Every few weeks some of us get together."

She looked at him. "So, you schedule time out from work for play?"

"I learned something growing up in a house with a man who chose to lose himself in paperwork and meetings. Leisure time is important. Important for balance. Important for symmetry. You need to stay focused, but…" He considered it more deeply. "Everyone, even great men, need to let go sometime."

A slight glitch in his controlled expression spoke to her

and she read between the lines. "Your father," she ventured. "He never got over your mother leaving, did he?"

What Tamara knew of De Luca Senior she didn't like. Without fail, his steely-eyed portrait sent a shudder up her vertebrae whenever she passed. Still, her romantic side couldn't deny a pang of sympathy. Perhaps Dante would have been less stern and uncompromising if his family life had been whole and happy. Bitterness could so easily grow from regret.

Armand's grin was wry. "My father loved her 'til the day he died. But while Angela was a beautiful woman, she was also something of a free spirit. When she left, my father couldn't convince her to return, no matter how hard he tried or what he threatened. He used to roar that her stubbornness would destroy him."

Destroy the family, Armand seemed to say as he yanked another dandelion from its nest. Angela not only left her husband, she'd also, for whatever reason, left behind her oldest son. As lacking as her own childhood had been, Tamara hadn't been abandoned, at least not by her mother.

She brought up her knees and hugged them. The more she learned about Armand, the more intrigued she became. "What were the circumstances surrounding your parents' marriage?"

His chin kicked up, but his eyes remained on the sea. "Circumstances?"

"Did they date for years? Was it a speedy romance?" Her stomach pitched. "Was she already pregnant before saying I do?"

He didn't move, not a lash. Armand was still but for his hair rumpling in the breeze.

Then he shifted his concentration back to the dandelions, waving a palm, like a magician, over their tops. "There's a lot to be said for accepting responsibility. But a person must also stand by it or there are consequences. A promise is sacrosanct. My mother refused to recognize that."

"She accepted your father's proposal, but didn't stand by their matrimonial vows. Is that what you mean?"

He gave a curt nod.

She hugged her legs tighter. His message was clear. Should they marry and it failed to work, Armand would fight to his last before agreeing to divorce. What an irony. Tamara couldn't shake off a rich man if she'd wanted to and her mother hadn't been able to keep or forget one.

Elaine Kendle had believed the man she loved would someday return and sweep her away from a life of drudgery. As Tamara's birthdays passed, her lack of understanding had grown. Her mother would have done better to invest in herself, but she'd scoffed at the idea of going back to school or getting a better job. Tamara had been determined not to repeat those mistakes, the biggest of all—loving a man who couldn't know the meaning of the word, for partner or for child.

Armand's words broke into her thoughts. "I don't want to discuss my parents, Tamara. I want to talk about us."

When his hand reached out, an electrical current sped up her legs and sparked low in her tummy, but still she hesitated to accept his contact. Cords shifted down his neck as he reached higher, cupping her cheek. The sparks raced up to zap her brain and confuse her more. Giving in—leaning in—her eyes drifted closed as intense longing soaked through her bloodstream.

Armand made her feel so defenseless, uncertain, yet at the same time so incredibly safe.

"This can work, Tamara. I have no doubt."

Her eyes opened to find his gaze dark and hot. Swallowing hard, she tried to think rationally, responsibly. She mustn't make the same mistakes.

"We haven't known each other even a month."

The pad of his thumb brushed her chin. "You can't be worried we won't be compatible. You like my company and enjoy when we kiss." The slant of his mouth was devilish. "I enjoy it, too."

Suddenly, even with the wind blustering overhead, she couldn't get enough air. She clasped her hands together in her lap and willed her muddled brain to work. "A kiss or two isn't enough to build a marriage on."

"Guess that depends on the kiss." His smiling eyes sobered. "But you're right. We need to be sure."

With a liquid movement, he found her shoulders and brought her down to lie beside him. Runaway heartbeats exploding through her chest, Tamara gasped as he gathered her close, nestling her crown beneath his chin. His palm shaped her body to his while his deep voice vibrated through to her bones. "How's the fit so far?"

When he nuzzled her brow and she absorbed more of his distinct male scent, her insides throbbed with an almost painful need. Unsure of what to say, only knowing she wanted to go forward, her hands carefully fanned between them to measure the solid frame of his chest. Pulse pounding in her ears, she peered up.

No warning. His mouth simply dropped over hers and she was lost, a victim of sensation, a slave to emotion. She'd waited for more of this contact—confirmation of her feelings, his desire—but until this moment, she hadn't realized how much.

While he massaged her hip, his tongue coaxed hers out. He suckled the tip and a delicious compression kicked off in her womb. When he shifted, altering the angle to deepen the caress, she became weightless, detached, floating above the world and beyond all care.

She'd never been kissed the way Armand kissed, with understated skill and relish. He released parts of her she hadn't realized existed but wanted so much to explore.

As the kiss eased off, her mouth shamelessly followed his. Rather than complying, he rolled her onto her back, shackling both wrists above her head while the waves crashed below and her body screamed out for more. Her core burned with want, beating a private rhythm her entire body ached to mime.

"Help me believe. Say you'll marry me, Tamara. I can't wait any longer."

When Armand retracted a small jewelry box from his pocket and presented her with the most beautiful ring— an exquisite ruby, which appeared to be the feminine partner to his masculine setting—Tamara couldn't speak.

"This ring is steeped in tradition," Armand told her.

"My paternal great-great grandfather had both rings made by the finest craftsman in Florence. The jewelry was handed down. Apparently a De Luca couple's future happiness is foretold by the woman's response when presented with this ring."

Senses swirling, she focused inward. As much as she tried to play devil's advocate and muddy it, the answer seemed clear. This intensity felt right. The ring was perfect. Destiny had brought them together. The sizzling through her veins, the passion and conviction in his voice…it must be the beginning. She believed in fate, in the way she felt cradled in his arms. How could she not believe in them?

Collecting all her courage, she slowly nodded.

"Yes."

He shifted and drilled her eyes, questioning before a flicker of what must be relief, or happiness, sped across his face. He slipped the ring on her finger then kissed her again, 'til her toes curled, her body hummed and her thinking was reduced to molasses.

He growled softly as his lips slipped languidly back and forth over hers and he reluctantly drew away. His seductive smile wrapped around and squeezed her very soul. "We need to set a date. How's a week from today."

Her stomach muscles contracted with nerves. Was it possible to organize everything at such short notice? Not only that, "Next Saturday is Christmas Eve."

He merely smiled. "So it is."

Shaking from what felt like shock, she twined her arms around the thick column of his neck. "I'd like to wear white."

A finger curled around a lock of her hair while his gaze embraced her. "You'll look fabulous in a white gown."

She imagined the endless list of guests who would hope for an invitation and felt a little overwhelmed. So shy in her early years, she'd always pictured her special day as a very private affair. "Can it be a small wedding?"

His grin tugged to one side. "Let's say smallish."

"Church weddings are beautiful…." She dragged her thoughts away from recent organ music and rushed on, "But can the ceremony be outside? I really like the idea of blue sky and the smell of summer roses."

He seemed about to nod, before his brows fell together. Snatching a look at the time, he cursed. "We'll discuss it tonight."

He sprang up, clasped her hand and eased her to unsteady feet. He folded the blanket as he strode toward the car. Realizing she hadn't followed, he snapped a gaze over one broad shoulder.

"You okay?" Crossing back, he dropped the blanket, held her upper arms and searched her face. "Do you feel dizzy?"

Tamara blew out the breath she'd been holding. She didn't feel dizzy or sick. More like…disappointed. These weeks had been such a buildup. Yet the moment she'd said yes, he had to rush off to a meeting. Maybe it was naive but she'd expected more.

Frowning, he scooped back the hair billowing like a dark veil over her head. The wind was stronger now, and cool.

He bent to swing her up. "I'll carry you to the car."

Pushing his shoulder, she stepped back. "I'm fine."

He was a busy, important executive. She'd known that all along. This is the way it would be, and she'd better get used to it. Besides, she'd have her own schedule when the baby came, as well as later when she returned to the business world.

One hand holding her hair, the other clutching her flapping skirt, she found an accommodating smile. "I'm just looking forward to tonight."

Grudgingly he accepted her excuse and collected the dropped blanket.

As they walked arm in arm to the Jag, chilly wind pushing at her back, she had a thought. "Can we go out to dinner?"

She wanted to celebrate and knew just the dress— long, elegant and dark. Armand would love it. And hopefully an evening alone would spark whatever was just lost.

"Excellent idea." Still walking, he stooped to press a kiss to her brow. "I won't be late."

CHAPTER FIVE

ARMAND entered his house that night after 9:00 p.m., still reeling. The meeting had not gone to plan. In fact, it had gone belly-up. Then there was the news he'd received afterward regarding Tamara, something completely out of left field and more prickly than a cactus. All in all, one hell of a day.

After tossing his keys on the foyer's antique centerpiece table—then tripping over one of its pain-in-the-butt colossal claw feet—he bit his lip, jammed a hand through his hair and tried to focus on the brighter side. Tamara had agreed to marry him. The baby would have the De Luca name, which, given the circumstances, was the best for all concerned.

As yet, no one outside this house knew about the pregnancy and he'd keep it that way 'til after the ceremony. The birth would occur within the time frame allotted by the will. He would win controlling interest of DLE without a hitch, despite the "Benedict Arnold" Matthew Mohill had slid in today.

Cursing, Armand strode toward his study. Extraordinary…until recently, when gut instinct had warned him otherwise, Matt had been the last person he would suspect of betrayal. He'd trusted his former confidant completely. But perhaps in some ways he should thank his father's old friend. A hard lesson, but when all was said and done, who in heaven and hell could a man trust.

Tamara's regal silhouette at the top of the stairs pulled Armand up short. His heart rate doubled at the sight of her. A pulse-beat later he drank in the incredible black sheath drawing his gaze down curves that had become increasingly tempting. A nanosecond after that, he remembered their date.

Damn!

Gaze bright with hurt, back straight, she began to descend. "I thought about phoning, but you were obviously tied up. I didn't want to disturb you."

Her tone was unclear. But contemptuous or sincere, nothing could be done. If his domestic memory had lapsed it was because he'd just endured one of the rockiest days of his life.

She reached him, that delicious dress and sway of ripening hips ridiculing him for keeping her waiting so long. Her dainty hand, jewelry-free, rested on the white balustrade. Her hair was swept to one side with a series of diamond and emerald clips he'd bought on a whim last week. The other side flowed like a satin river over a shoulder. Her fragrance was subtle yet intoxicating enough to almost make him forget the pack of problems nipping at his heels.

He shoved both hands in his pockets, felt that note buried at the bottom of one and smothered a cringe. "I was held up."

Her glossy lips quaked as she attempted a smile. "Are you hungry? Would you like a sandwich? Ruth made a pile before she left—" she hesitated "—just in case."

He wasn't hungry. He needed a scotch, and some way to mend the gaping knife wound in his back. From the balustrade he took Tamara's cool hand, which tonight felt as fragile as a sparrow's wing, and led her down the wide, dimly lit hall.

The click-clacking of her heels on the marble floor echoed off the walls. "Want to talk about it?"

The sting eased a fraction at her commonsense attitude. Yes, she was a romantic, but now they'd made a commitment, it seemed he could rely on her support. His father had said many times that duty in a wife was a busy man's best friend, and a willful woman a husband's worst nightmare.

At the study door he paused, but continued on to their favorite room. He'd already spent too many hours behind a desk today.

He helped her down onto what he now viewed as "Tamara's couch," engrossed in the way that goddess of a gown pooled around her daintily aligned feet. After pouring himself a drink, he offered her some ice water, then flopped into the familiar comfort of his wing chair. "There's been a development."

She peered over her tumbler, the flushed color draining from her cheeks. "You don't want to marry me."

The statement was so absurd he had trouble digesting it. "Of course I want to marry you."

In fact, the idea had taken on a life all its own. Taking his time to woo Tamara had been more pleasurable, and difficult, than he'd imagined. The anticipation of finally enjoying her affections had spiraled to an agonizing crescendo. But he'd resisted long enough to ensure she would succumb today, and eagerly so. Now the gates to paradise were open.

While he sipped and contemplated, Tamara let out a breath and rolled her eyes at her misunderstanding. "Guess this big empty house got the better of me."

"Won't be so empty in six months time."

A new and pleasant warmth bathed his senses. This was actually happening. He'd put together hundreds of deals but until this moment, this significant turn in his life hadn't seemed real. Tamara was having a baby and he would be the father, in practice and in name.

More De Luca children would follow, offspring to carry on the line and legacy, descendants of his seed. He would make certain the path leading to their future was better laid than his and Marco's had been. No loopholes with trust. No broken families. Every *t* crossed, every *i* dotted. He'd start implementing measures as soon as possible.

"I've been thinking about names."

Tamara's comment brought him back from deliberations over his own will. "Baby names?" She nodded and Armand's chest inflated with pride. "It's a tradition that the firstborn's middle name be Daniele. A strong boy's name."

Her full lips tilted. "Who says it's a boy?"

Armand's mind flew in a circle. He hadn't considered the possibility. Medical fact stated men decide gender, and De Luca firstborns had been male from the dawn of his family history. Still he supposed there was no guarantee, and he wasn't inflexible.

He tasted his scotch, considering. "If it's a girl the middle name will be Daniela."

Her expression froze then she blinked. "I'm not sure I want that."

He arched a brow. "Oh?"

Her silver heels slipped off and long legs winged up beside her. "I was thinking Georgia or maybe Paige."

He chuckled and settled deeper into his chair. "They're not Italian names."

"I'm not Italian."

"I am."

"Only half."

"The half that matters."

Her legs came down. "What's that supposed to mean?"

His head cocked. She couldn't be upset, merely looking for answers. As her future husband, he was happy to provide her with as many as she needed. "It means it's fitting that we follow tradition."

"And if I don't like tradition?"

Rotating his glass, he quietly reminded her, "We've had this discussion."

"Really? When?"

"Marriage is an old-fashioned and serious institution." He offered a charitable look. "A couple should be mindful of that."

"You mean a wife should be mindful of her husband."

He mentally shook his head. Her mouth was no longer tilted; it was tight. Where had the understanding companion gone? Given the steam shooting from the shell of her diamond-drop ear, guess that issue needed to be tabled for a future date.

Either way, the child's middle name was decided. Tamara would come to accept it, just as she'd come to accept him. However, for now, a change of subject might be best.

He set his glass upon the walnut side table and, elbows on rests, clasped his hands to form a bridge. "I thought you wanted to know about my day."

Acid rose in his gut, but the dilemma couldn't be ignored. Irrespective of this mix-up over names, Tamara would soon be his wife. She should hear the news from him. The boardroom news, in any case. He hadn't decided what to do about the other.

"Today Matthew voted against me."

She sat slowly back as if all the air had left her. "Against your motion to expand into Asia?"

The muscles at either side of his nape pinched. Exercising his neck with a roll, he pushed to his feet. "I went through the preliminary figures, the projections for lead time and expenditure versus profit. He waited 'til I'd finished then calmly announced that, given his independent research, it was a risky and unnecessary move."

"After all I've heard about your past, how close you've been," she said, her beautiful face flooded with sympathy, "that must have been a shock."

Matthew's behavior had certainly burned. Last time Armand had felt this betrayal was over a woman. Never again would he endure a trampled heart; that naive pocket of his character was sealed forever. Damn straight no one would play him for a fool over DLE again, either.

"There was no need to continue with the pretense of a vote," he went on. "Matthew's arrow split them down the middle. It'll take watertight strategy to regroup and swing them around now."

Which would have to come after the full release of the financial year figures. He had no choice. He needed to make the healthy company profit work to his advantage in this matter and convince them to be proactive rather than overriding the crest of a wave. New angles, new opportunities, new ways of thinking—that was how to stay on top.

Glass in hand, Tamara eased up, the fall of her gown swishing around her bare feet as she walked toward him.

"I'm sorry, Armand. It's hard when a friend doesn't agree."

His chin pulled in. Little wonder her business had crashed; he truly shouldn't feel responsible for the information scrawled on the note in his pocket. Clearly Tamara couldn't interpret warning signs when corporate push needed to come to unapologetic shove.

"Matthew and I could have discussed any concerns before three o'clock today." Setting his jaw, he gazed, unseeing, at a gilt-framed Monet mounted on the far wall. "This wasn't about compromise. He wanted to throw the gauntlet down."

At his side now, Tamara's soft floral scent worked to soothe his aggravated senses. God, how he wished this conversation was over so they could get back to where they'd left off this afternoon and simply fall into bed.

"Matthew wants to challenge you?" she asked. "Why?"

Armand could guess. "Before the meeting, he showed off a photo of his bride. I'd expected someone around his age, a sweet dear with a blue rinse. Evie Mohill is your age, a Nordic beauty and, evidently, ambitious."

"You think she's convinced him to undermine your authority?"

"And, possibly, try to keep controlling interest of my company."

Tamara's earring winked in the room's muted light as she laughed. "Surely Matthew wouldn't jeopardize your friendship because his wife of a few weeks is a gold digger. No intelligent, already wealthy man would do it." She wrapped one arm across her waist, rested an elbow on the wrist and positioned her glass for another sip. "You must be wrong."

Armand's deliberations grew darker. He looked at Tamara but saw Matthew's tanned face and pale eyes evaluating him across the board table earlier today. His pulse throbbed up his throat, booming at his temples as his agitation increased. "I'm not wrong. But you may be right."

Her hair cascaded as she set her glass on an occasional table. "Now you're talking in riddles."

"I know Matthew as well as I knew my father. I saw it in his eyes, Tamara. He didn't hang around to discuss it afterward. He intends to move against me. But, I think you're dead-on. He wouldn't throw in all his chips solely to satisfy a woman, even one he so obviously adores." No thinking man would. "There's more to it. But I doubt he'll provide the rest of the puzzle 'til he believes he has another advantage."

She slowly exhaled as if unsure of how to help, then gave his sleeve a comforting stroke. "You won't be able to sleep tonight."

"Probably not." Inspired by her touch, he wove her into the fabric of a meaningful embrace and his blood began to heat and stir. "But at least I'll be pleasantly distracted for a good part of it."

Lifting her chin with a crooked finger, he tasted the seam of her slightly parted mouth and the outer layers of his troubles began to loosen and shed. His left hand shimmied up her outside thigh. As waves of silk built above his hand, she trembled and leaned closer.

Standing front to front, her breasts pressed against his ribs, he pictured their peaks—delicate rosy-tipped beads. When he imagined how they'd feel pushing against his palms, rolling over his tongue, he decided it was time to adjourn upstairs.

"Armand…I want to wait."

Her words, a ragged whisper brushed against his cheek, held him back. Wait to make love? Grinning, he nuzzled into her neck. "'Til after dinner?" He had no appetite for anything but her.

"'Til our wedding night."

He flinched as his surroundings creaked and warped. His grip on her shoulders tightened even as he audibly scoffed. She was teasing. Had to be.

His hands skimmed over the crests of her shoulders, down her smooth bare back before scooping in her bottom so she fit snuggly against him. Her answering sigh hummed through every channel of his consciousness, 'til all he knew was the throbbing beat of his physical need. Now was not the time for games, unless they were the bedroom variety.

He rocked her oh-so-gently then, unashamedly focused on her mouth, slow-danced her back toward the couch. "The wedding's a week away."

"I want it to be right."

His impulse hardened and grew. "Oh, it'll be one hundred percent."

The back of her knees met the couch and he eased her down, an arm supporting her back as she lay.

"Then you understand."

Her apologetic yet firm tone tapped like a cracking egg on his brain. Poised above her, one knee embedded beside her far hip, the other foot on the carpet, his gaze followed his hand trailing the flow of her naked arm. His mouth joined hers, his attentions more insistent this time. They were both breathless and steaming when he reluctantly pulled back to slip the spaghetti strap from her shoulder. "Understand…about what?"

She caught his hand. "About holding off."

The leg supporting his weight almost buckled. He stared down at her…that kissable mouth and smooth edible throat, terrain he craved to vanquish and make his own.

Tonight.

His voice was a husky plea. "You're not serious."

"Wouldn't you rather wait, too?"

He rubbed his temple.

Her gaze was wounded. "You were the one to spout off about the importance of tradition."

A sinking feeling, like a dropped missile, sailed right through him. Armand groaned and put her logic together. "Therefore I should want to consummate our marriage on our wedding night and not before." Dammit, he'd trapped himself.

She framed his face between her hands, her gaze pleading. "Everything has been so rushed. I want our first night together to really mean something."

He was tempted to promise that it would. But her glistening eyes spoke to him at a level that existed beyond lust, and his more noble side stepped up to thrust the howling beast aside. He'd waited this long, knowing eventually his kind of justice would prevail. He would marry and in six months present to the world a legitimate heir to satisfy the will's obligations.

Where along the way had the lines blurred? A successful seduction was supposed to help achieve those goals, not become his paramount objective.

Besides, dammit, Tamara was right. Once they joined, their union would be forever. No turning back or running away from commitment, for either of them. Although every male fiber urged him to convince and claim her now, this wasn't some heat-of-the-moment sexual conquest. This meant future…family. For that, he could wait.

Sucking down a calming breath, he found his feet and hauled her up. "It's getting late. You must be tired. We'll go to dinner tomorrow night. I'll walk you to your room."

Now she looked like a wide-eyed child who'd discovered her name wasn't on any of the presents under the tree. Mother of mercy! Now was not the time to play with matches. If he kissed her again, he doubted he could control the inferno.

Muscles locked, he turned toward his chair and, determined now his mind was made up, stamped down the last of the sparking tinder. "Perhaps I should stay here."

An uncomfortable silence stretched out, before she murmured in a resigned but hardly contented tone, "Perhaps you should. Good night, Armand."

Nodding, he sent a quick tight smile and let her leave the room before sinking back onto the couch. When he was sure she was gone, he retracted the note from his pocket, which his secretary must have left on his desk sometime Friday, but he'd discovered only after today's meeting—the icing on the cake, so to speak.

He unfolded the paper and gazed at the message.

Wanting to impress, his P.I. had dug a little deeper. Seemed Tamara's bankruptcy could have been avoided. Payment of that outstanding invoice had been held up unnecessarily. If she'd pushed a little harder, been dogged and resolute, she would have prevailed and shot out the other side into solvency.

He'd brought home the note half convinced he might reveal this recently unearthed information, but, clearly, passing this on would help no one. Hindsight wasn't merely useless—at this delicate point in time, it could prove lethal.

He pushed up and moved to a cedar writing table tucked into a corner where the room's yellow light barely touched, and from its single drawer retrieved his father's pipe lighter. Crossing to the wet bar, he flipped the lighter's catch and the note's edge danced into flame. His ruby ring flashed as he dropped the burning paper onto a silver tray and watched it crackle and curl in on itself 'til it was black and unsalvageable.

The charred fumes ate at his lungs and stung his eyes, but he stared until the bones were cool before washing the remains down the sink. Finally he crossed to the doorway and clicked off the dimmer switch.

His conscience pricked as he closed the door, but he'd taken the only sound course of action. They were starting a new life and needed to set off on the right foot; tonight Tamara had confirmed she wanted that, too. She need never know about the incompetence surrounding her business's demise, or that the company responsible—Barclays Australasia, the entity that could still make amends—was owned by DLE.

She might wrongly assume he'd known about this before now and withheld the money to increase his advantage. She might even call off the engagement, and that was not an option. This situation needed to be buried.

In a week's time his goal would be achieved and she need never worry again. The will issue would be settled, Tamara would be his and they would be a family unit. At her truest level she would have to agree…that was all that mattered.

CHAPTER SIX

TAPPING her pen at the meals table she sometimes used as a homework desk, Tamara pushed aside her toast to concentrate on the numeric scrawl taunting her from the opened textbook.

Hovering beside her, Armand finished straightening his aqua silk tie. "Having trouble with the assignment?"

"You could say that." Although "headed down the gurgler" sounded more like it.

"This the last one?"

Enjoying his forest-fresh scent, she took in the chiseled planes of his face. A couple of days ago she'd agreed to be this man's wife yet their betrothal still seemed like some fantastic dream.

Redirecting her gaze, she pushed out a sigh and doodled a *C* on her pad. "Results for the last assignment were up on the university site this morning. I passed."

Thank heaven. But the modules were getting tougher. Then there was the exam and two final units first semester next year. So close and yet so far.

He crouched beside her, his big tanned hand a toasty oven over hers. The contact, as well as the proximity of his mouth and newly shaven jaw, didn't help her concentration one bit. Nothing new. He aroused her simply by being near.

His hand squeezed hers. "Maybe you should give it a break until after the baby's born. You don't want to push yourself too hard."

A band around her chest tightened as she slid her hand from under his. "I'm struggling a little," she downplayed, "but finishing this degree is important to me."

He found her hand again. "Your well-being is important to *me*."

His touch reassured her, but his adamant tone ruffled her feathers. Gaze reverting to her books, she shook her head. "You don't understand."

Her reasons might not be unique, but they stemmed from the kind of past Armand could never grasp. Every time her mother had pinned up her graying hair and slumped off for another long laundry shift, Tamara reaffirmed her vow: Hell's flames would turn into a blizzard before she'd slip into her mother's worn and weary shoes. Education and determination were two ways to ensure that.

"I understand," he said, "that you felt you needed to do this, but your situation has changed."

Nonplussed, she shrugged. "See?"

He opened each of her curled fingers then pressed her palm to his lips. "See what?"

A rush of star-tipped tingles swirled up her arm. Did he have to distract her like that during a serious discussion? This was important.

Wanting to keep this private, she flicked a glance toward the kitchen, but Ruth had left the room. Tamping down the remaining tingles, she met his gaze and repeated, "You don't understand."

Still crouched, he angled closer and joined his mouth to hers. No embrace to hold her close; his animal magnetism was enough to keep her glued. As his tongue worked with hers, heat flared in her middle then spread like quicksilver through her body, 'til her ears burned and insides pulsed.

Too soon, the kiss trailed off. Close to melting, she inwardly groaned as he pulled away.

The curve of his hand trailed her face. "In a few days you will be married to one of the country's wealthiest men. You won't have to worry about anything again. I'll see to it."

Tamara drifted back down to earth to collect her thoughts. Men of Armand's breed solved problems their way—by advancing, protecting and taking ultimate responsibility. In theory, noble qualities that might make a woman feel delicate and precious. But she was more than chattel.

"This isn't about landing a rich man, then living a privileged life. Finishing this degree is about who I was and what I always wanted to achieve."

His lazy gaze seemed to sympathize as his thumb rubbed her wrist. "I always wanted a family. I assumed you wanted one, too."

"A fresh cup before you leave, sir?"

While Tamara caught the breath she'd lost, Armand, infuriatingly composed, glanced over at Ruth, who had returned and looked set to hand-beat a chocolate muffin mix at the counter.

"Thanks, Ruth—" he snatched a look at his watch "—but I'm running late."

As if understanding, Master grizzled and scrambled from his navy-colored toweling mat laid out near the French doors. He knocked his coconut-sized head under his best friend's elbow. Armand obliged with a ruffle then sprang up. His six-foot-plus height, the breadth and depth of his chest…Armand was built like a tower no one could threaten and nothing could topple. A modern-day corporate warrior…

Who wanted a family.

Initially she believed his objective in marrying her was based solely on expediency, blended with obligation; he needed an heir and had subsequently decided her baby needed his name. But just now he made having a family together sound so natural, even fated, as if they'd talked about it every other Sunday for a year.

"I've looked into obstetricians," he said, tossing Master a piece of croissant from his vacated plate. "Dr. Fielding isn't taking new clients, but she's the best. I'll get an appointment before the wedding."

That air of authority again. But on the heels of his always-wanted-a-family statement, frankly, his manner now made her feel less like a chattel and more like a lady with her knight. Still, there was no need to bust down the good doctor's door. "My GP checked me out late last week. Everything's fine."

Although she hadn't much liked the blood samples she'd given for some tests her doctor had suggested. She didn't like needles—not the sting so much as the mere thought.

Armand's expression as he patted his hands on a napkin said he'd do what he deemed best. "I'll be home early."

His eyes twinkled, but a ghost of some other emotion, an echo from an earlier conversation, dulled the sparkle. She'd seen that set of his jaw many times since her request that they wait until their wedding night. He hadn't been happy about the delay in taking their intimate relationship to a sizzling summit, but she had to give him credit. Even when she had had second thoughts, he'd remained within limits.

Oh, there'd been plenty of embracing and kissing, like a moment ago, or in the pool. The mix of hard muscle, cool water and hot passion never failed to leave her a quivering, syrupy mess. But before their mounting friction could combust, he leapt out of the water, lashed a giant towel around his washboard waist and strode directly to the shower. No need to guess why. He wanted her. Bad. God, how she wanted him, too.

Armand headed for the counter, where his black leather briefcase waited. "You haven't thought of anyone else you'd like to invite?"

Married. I'm getting married.

And on Christmas Eve. Prepared as always, Armand had lodged the required paperwork before she'd even accepted. Presumptuous, but she hadn't complained.

"I contacted everyone on my list yesterday." Her contribution to the numbers comprised maybe a dozen people. All had been home and said yes, except one.

"No one from your school days, or your old neighborhood?"

She supposed she could invite a couple of nice neighbors and some acquaintances from the Exemplar Events days. But it was such short notice. Besides, she looked forward to seeing only those people she truly wanted to help celebrate their day, including her mother.

Tamara hoped Elaine Kendle would reply. Their phone conversations were down to a three or four a year, but this could be a fresh start. They had the best reason to forget their barren past. Elaine would be a grandmother soon.

"I want to prepare you," Armand said, swinging his case off the counter. "Matthew will be there."

Tamara spluttered in her raspberry tea. "I thought you two were arguing."

He raised a brow. "It's much worse than that."

"Then why are you inviting him?"

"Have you heard the phrase 'keep your friends close and your enemies closer'?" He took a mouthful from a cup Ruth had poured anyway. "Besides I don't want to inflame the idea of a widening rift. Many of the board members are coming and will expect Matthew to be there, too."

Tamara nibbled her toast. Armand and Matthew had been friends for so long. Surely that kind of bond didn't wash away overnight. Matthew had been as good as family. If she was willing to try with her mother, surely Armand could try with him.

She set her toast down. "I think it's a good idea

Matthew's coming. It might be the opportunity you both need to sit down outside of the office and work out what's really eating you."

Armand cocked his head, half-amused. "Believe me. Matthew doesn't want understanding or forgiveness. He has a broader agenda. This is business, Tamara. Big business."

Perhaps, but… "Isn't it personal, too?" she asked.

He sauntered toward her. "Business is always personal."

The glint in Armand's eyes suggested something more. If business was personal, perhaps the reverse was true: the personal was always business.

She avoided his gaze as her palm settled over the twinge in her tummy,

Since saying yes, she'd convinced herself a little more each day that Armand's cynicism regarding love was waning and they might actually be falling in love. But maybe she was kidding herself. Maybe she was still merely the practical choice for the family he had not only always wanted, but now also needed.

Binding legal papers would soon be signed. If she married only to discover later that his attentions were more about achieving goals than true affection, she couldn't pull out. Armand would fight tooth and nail before he'd let her, or his heir, leave, which begged another sensitive question.

Would he love this baby as much as she did…as he would his own child when it came along?

Briefcase in hand, Armand bent to say goodbye and she simply couldn't help it; the doubts magically disappeared. All she knew was the steady stir of longing as his mouth settled over hers.

He rubbed her nose with his. "I'll see you tonight," he murmured in a husky voice. Then, every inch the sexy CEO in his dark Armani suit, he strode off to disappear through the door adjoining the multicar garage.

Thankfully Ruth was there to fill the void.

The housekeeper's tray rattled into the oven. "How about a muffin when they're done?"

The aroma of freshly baked chocolate sponge rose up to claim Tamara's imagination but she wasn't tempted. "Maybe midmorning."

Ruth removed her red-patterned oven mitts and slotted them into her apron's side-to-side front pocket. "Would you like a glass of milk to settle your tummy?"

Tamara smiled. "Don't worry. No morning sickness. I'm just not hungry."

At thirteen weeks gestation, the worst of the hunger pangs had passed. She felt healthier, and a little heavier, each day. But while weight gain might be a necessary part of pregnancy, her doctor had suggested that appropriate exercise was important, too.

She clapped shut her books and stood. "In fact, a walk might work up an appetite." It would be good to get out in the sunshine and enjoy the silky fragrance of the roses in bloom beyond the courtyard.

Wearing delicate pearl earrings today, Ruth crossed to collect the breakfast dishes. "Nice time of day, before it gets too hot. But take your hat."

Tamara wanted to hug her. Between Ruth and Armand, she felt wrapped in the finest cotton wool.

"I'll take my books, too. The view might inspire my brain to work."

"Want a rug to sit on?"

"I think I'll camp out on the bench next to the statue."

Dishes in hand, Ruth moved to the sink. "Mrs. De Luca liked sitting out there, too."

Reaching for her books, Tamara snapped around. "You knew Angela?" Ruth had been here a long time, but over twenty-five years?

Ruth's usually straight bearing sagged slightly as she flicked on the faucet. "I thought about leaving after the trouble. But I couldn't when…" She visibly shuddered. "Well, you know."

"No, Ruth, I don't know. Armand doesn't like to discuss his parents."

Ruth's mouth thinned. "Understandable."

Now the door was open, Tamara couldn't let it close without finding out what lay behind. At times she felt close to knowing Armand, at others he seemed a complete enigma, which might have its benefits in the commercial world, but wasn't so great between future man and wife.

"Tell me, Ruth. What happened?"

Avoiding the question, Ruth switched on the oven light and stooped to check the muffins' progress. "It's really not my place to say."

"I know sometimes a woman is given, or is left with no choice," Tamara said. "But why would someone in Angela's position choose to leave behind a child?"

Ruth wheeled around. "She didn't leave him behind. Dante wouldn't let her take him."

More puzzled than ever, Tamara sank back into her chair. "Yet he let her take his younger son?"

"It wasn't like that, either." Uneasy, Ruth shoveled both hands into her apron pocket and flapped. "The story's complicated."

"I bet it is." Tamara sat forward, hands clasped before her. She didn't want to push, but something close to her heart said she should. This was important and she wouldn't find out from Armand. She gave Ruth an imploring look.

Ruth flapped the apron once more then, on a groan, reluctantly nodded.

"At the start, it was ideal," she explained, walking slowly forward. "They were very happy, Dante already wealthy beyond belief, Angela from more humble beginnings. Angela breezed through the first pregnancy, but took a few months to adjust after Marco. She was…listless, I suppose the word is. She loved her babies but said she felt lost in this huge house all day. She used to say she was a feather wafting around in a big empty maze."

Lost. That word pretty much summed up the restlessness Tamara suffered whenever Armand was gone. The feeling had been the same when she was younger, too, left home alone hours on end. Maybe it was more about floating in a kind of limbo, waiting endlessly—it sometimes seemed—for someone who wasn't necessarily waiting for you.

Ruth lowered down into a chair. "Mr. De Luca tried to understand. He organized charity events for her to attend, hired a lovely nanny who was available anytime

Angela needed." Ruth blinked down and took hold of the rumpled napkin. "Then Angela hinted at returning to part-time nursing."

Armand had used the term *free spirit* when they'd spoken briefly about his mother; Tamara had pictured a painter or dancer, perhaps a fragile type like Ophelia in *Hamlet*. Had he, and his father, thought Angela a free spirit simply because she wanted to find some fulfillment outside of the home?

Elbows on thighs, Tamara brought her threaded hands under her chin. "What kind of nursing?"

"Accident and emergency. Takes special talent, so I'm told. And she desperately missed doing what she loved—helping mend people, many times saving them. While Mr. De Luca was at work, she brushed up on her qualifications. There was all hell to pay when he found out."

"Why?" But Tamara suspected the answer.

"He said she didn't need to work. A mother's job was to look after the children, and a wife's was to look after her husband. He lost his parents young," she added, by way of apology. "Had to work very hard to keep anything he earned."

The smear of empathy Tamara felt didn't erase the queasiness stewing low in her stomach. "Dante had very old-fashioned ideas." About wills, about women, she thought.

Ruth kneaded the napkin like a knob of dough. "He was traditional, yes, indeed." She met Tamara's gaze. "But things were different back then."

Was Dante's son so different now? Armand had been

raised in a house where the man's opinion was the only one that counted. Hell, he even accepted Dante's reasons for including that ridiculous clause in his will. She'd been taken aback, but not overly alarmed, when Armand assumed he would decide the medical specialist and baby's name.

Perhaps after the wedding he'd decide she shouldn't pursue her own interests, her education, her business. She couldn't really imagine him being that chauvinistic. Then again, Angela probably hadn't, either.

Ruth heaved out a sigh. "The more Dante put his foot down, the more determined Angela became. She took a part-time position and terrible arguments followed. One day when she was in her car leaving to take Marco to soccer training, Dante hurled an ultimatum at her. Stay and be a mother to both, he said, or leave with the one you have."

Tamara flinched as a frantic scene unfolded in her mind.

"He wouldn't allow her back until she surrendered," Ruth went on. "She tried to make him see reason, but he put Armand in a boarding school and served court orders against her removing him. Cited negligence as the reason. She called him a devil and fought to get access to Armand, but Dante's bullheadedness only grew and eventually turned his heart to pure stone. No one was allowed to mention her name."

"But how could he give up his younger son?" Marc was so special as an adult; he would have been a dimpled blond cherub as a child.

"When he realized Angela wouldn't return, Dante convinced himself Marco wasn't his. Even cut him from his inheritance. Angela had loved Dante. She'd been with no one else. But he wanted to control her, like he controlled everything. In trying to possess her, he only succeeded in pushing her farther away."

With a sorrowful air, Ruth threw the napkin at the bowl of fruit, and, as if pressing a button, the telephone rang. As Ruth eased up to answer it, Tamara let her joined hands drop between her knees.

What a heartrending story. A family destroyed, two little boys deprived of a parent's support and love. No wonder Marc and now Armand would rather let it rest.

But she wasn't sorry she'd prodded Ruth into explaining. Angela's misery couldn't be undone, but it was a blinking light for Tamara to bring forward her own concerns. Surely Armand wasn't as merciless as his father, even given his ruthless business reputation. Still, hearing this tragic tale settled it.

They'd get a few things straight before walking down the aisle. Maybe she should suggest a prenuptial agreement outlining what was expected of both parties. As an astute businessman, he should appreciate her diligence. If he balked at the idea…

Tamara unfolded to her feet.

Well, she'd just have to take it from there.

She was assembling her books, and her jumble of thoughts, when Ruth returned with the handheld phone. "Tamara, dear, it's your doctor."

A rush of sensation funneled from her stomach to her soles. She hadn't expected any communication. The doctor assured her everything was routine and she would see her in a month's time.

Thinking it through, Tamara chided herself and took the phone.

No doubt she'd left behind her health care card. Or maybe she needed another blood test. She shuddered. She *really* hated needles.

She grabbed the phone and listened eagerly. The conversation was brief and clinical, barring the "I'm so sorry" tagged on the end. Tamara couldn't think of a single thing to say. Everything seemed frozen. Her mind. Her voice. Surely this was some kind of joke.

Perhaps she said goodbye before the phone slipped from her hand. The clatter as it hit the tiles ricocheted in her ears at the same time Ruth's baking tray scraped from its oven rack. At her feet, Master licked a callus on his front paw before he looked up at her, his eyes so sad and uncomprehending. And all the while Tamara's throat burned, clogged with suffocating coals.

If she didn't give in to the tears backed up behind her eyes, perhaps this wouldn't be real. Perhaps God would let her go back in time and—

She barely noticed her shoulders being shaken.

Finally Ruth's voice penetrated the shock. "What's wrong? Tamara, look at me!"

She didn't want to. Didn't want to do anything but crumple up and hide from this heartbreaking news. But she made herself answer.

"The baby." Oh, dear Lord. "Something's wrong with the baby."

CHAPTER SEVEN

FORTY-FIVE minutes later, Tamara sat as stiff as a wax figure in the sterile office of the east coast's most respected obstetrician. Beside her, in the second guest chair, was Armand.

His hand squeezed hers repeatedly as he stared dead ahead at the empty chair behind the desk, and higher to the neat patchwork of degrees and credentials on the stark white wall.

His voice was firm, low and completely in charge. "Everything will be fine. Don't worry."

After the phone call, Tamara had suffered a delayed reaction before she'd sobbed like she never had before. Coolheaded Ruth had phoned Armand. He'd told her, since he was already in the city, a cab would be quicker for her.

She felt turned inside out, a wretched and drained mess. Her eyes burned as if they'd been dropped in a bucket of acid. Waiting for Dr. Fielding was tantamount to torture. She needed details. Needed to know if it was as bad as her GP had said.

Or worse.

"I'm so afraid."

She hadn't meant to speak aloud. It was clear from Armand's strained expression that he saw terror racing across her face, and he was right. Panic crawled up her spine and crushed her throat 'til she thought she might scream.

He leaned over and his lips brushed her hair. "Whatever it is, whatever it costs, no matter where we have to go, or who we have to see, the baby will be fine. Don't worry." He pressed a lingering kiss to her temple. "I'm right here."

"She said…" Tamara swallowed the nausea on the back of her tongue. "The doctor said there was a nine-in-ten chance of a major problem. That I'd have to make decisions."

She'd replayed the conversation over and over in her mind. The doctor said they'd need to do more tests. And make decisions. Decisions. What the hell was that supposed to mean?

She didn't want to know. The lunacy and injustice of it all left her bewildered. "I didn't stop to think about anything going wrong. I only ever saw my baby as perfect, to me…to the world."

"He will be." Armand didn't quite look at her as his nostrils flared. "I'll make certain of it."

So confident, so uncompromising. But she saw the sheen on his brow, the way his other hand gripped the armrest as if letting go meant dropping into an infinite abyss. They were together in this…in hope, in despair. He was here for her and her child.

Their child.

Tamara leaned back and stared at the ceiling, her body feverish, her insides strung high and tight.

Please, please, let this be over. Let it be all right.

She jumped when the swinging door pushed open. An attractive middle-aged woman, with honey-colored hair caught in a low ponytail at her back, swept into the room. Her gaze, behind frameless glasses, didn't leave the clear plastic folder she held until she'd settled in behind the desk. As though she'd only now sensed her guests' presence, her head pivoted up, the folder fell and the glasses were removed.

"I'm glad we were able to fit you in on such short notice, Ms. Kendle." She acknowledged Armand and nodded. "Mr. De Luca."

Armand ground out a reply. "Thank you for your time, Dr. Fielding."

Tamara wondered again at the influence Armand must wield to have plucked an appointment with this specialist out of thin air. But at this point, she didn't care how he'd managed it. Dr. Marion Fielding was the best. Her baby needed the best.

Lacing her hands on the teak desk, Dr. Fielding directed her words at Tamara. "I obtained the triple screen results from your GP, Ms. Kendle. I won't beat around the bush. There was an error with regard to the gestational age, which I know must have caused you both a great deal of pain."

Heart pumping, Tamara analyzed the doctor's sympathetic expression and tried to digest the impossible, wonderful news.

"You're thirteen weeks pregnant?" Dr. Fielding

asked. Tamara could only nod as the beginnings of tingling relief dripped through her bloodstream. "Your GP administered a test that offers the best results when conducted between sixteen and eighteen weeks." She flicked the folder with the back of her hand. "These results are abnormal and a concern only if you were further along. At thirteen weeks, however, the hormone levels are quite normal. There are other tests that can be conducted. I'll perform a scan. But to my mind," she said, smiling encouragingly, "there's no reason to expect anything other than a healthy baby in approximately six months time."

Tamara melted into the chair. The horror worse than death had been only a nightmare. She could wake up now.

"Thank you, Dr. Fielding." Armand surged up with the energy of a fireball.

Lighter than mist, Tamara followed. She shook the doctor's hand once Armand had freed it. "You can't imagine—" She exhaled on an ear-to-ear grin. "Imagine the relief."

Dr. Fielding's light brown eyes shone as though she might have a very good idea. "I'll have my receptionist book you in for your next checkup."

Tamara stood in a dreamy endorphin-rush daze as Armand finalized her next appointment at the desk. They were descending in the lift when she turned to him and blurted out, "You were right."

He turned to her, his handsome face supportive, a subtle smile tugging one corner of his mouth. "Right about what?"

"I should have listened. From the beginning you

wanted me to see the very best. But I fobbed it off, needing to play Miss Independence and do it on my own. I was stupid." She let her forehead drop against the hot wall of his jacketed chest. "All this pain, and it could have been avoided."

Her head rolled from side to side as she silently cursed herself. Foolish pride. Growing up she'd learned to rely on no one but herself. Her existence had been a lonely, sometimes frightening one. But it was high time to put those fears behind her.

Unfortunate circumstances had brought her and Armand together, but fate hadn't turned its back completely. Her business, her house, her dearest friend were all gone. But as recompense she had the most precious baby growing inside of her. And beside her was the man who had vowed to care for them both. Her greatest wish, which had seemed so elusive only weeks ago, was becoming a reality.

Driven by an overwhelming impulse, she bounced onto her toes and threw herself around his neck. He wound his arms around her middle and a profound sense of destiny doused and soothed her. His low chuckle, a deep luscious throaty sound, soaked in to salve and lift her even higher—not only from today's hellish descent, but also from her past.

His unique male scent filled her lungs. God, she loved how he smelled. Even more she loved how he felt, like a rock she could hang onto no matter how fierce the storm.

She murmured against the shell of his ear. "I should have trusted you, and let you make some decisions about the baby." He was going to be her child's father, for heaven's sake. But she hadn't truly accepted that… not until now.

For a heartbeat he stiffened, then his nose and mouth nestled in her hair. "It's okay. It's over now."

She trusted him. The revelation was like a white searing flare going off in her mind. She didn't need to talk to him about prenups. They need never talk about his parents, if he didn't want to. This man would never hurt or stifle her.

She was wise enough to admit that he'd been someone else when they'd met, a man driven by a cast of personal demons who had pushed him to succeed. But he wasn't carved from stone. Their evolving relationship had turned him around inch by inch. Today she felt that epiphany more deeply than the wild thumping of her heart.

"Don't get me anything for Christmas," she whispered, still huddled close, eyes shut deliciously tight as the lift whirred down. "I don't need or want a thing, other than to know we'll all be together next year."

He drew back, his eyes somber and dark, a single line etched between his brows. He stroked her chin before tugging her close. He kissed her with a tenderness that brought tears to her eyes. She knew she was still emotional from the scene in Dr. Fielding's office, but her reaction wasn't about that. A simple touch was enough to release butterflies in her stomach and send her heartbeat clattering like maracas. Yet this sensation was more than physical reaction. It was pure and meant to be.

No doubts now. She was falling in love with him. Arms spread wide, smile splitting her face, plummeting in love with Armand.

All the air in the lift had evaporated by the time his mouth finally left hers. Dizzy, and so happy, she wanted to go back and have his spell transport her again. But the metallic doors had already opened. The crowd gathered on the other side, gazing in with fawning smiles, meant this ride was over.

Or had only just begun.

CHAPTER EIGHT

THE DRIVE home took less than half an hour. Every minute, Tamara had burrowed into him like a purring Cheshire cat. Once in a while he dropped a kiss on her brow. He'd never felt so fiercely protective of a person. Of two people. Thank God, the test results had been wrong.

He was fond of Tamara, exceedingly so. She was sexy and witty. Coupled with her workable balance of individuality and compliance, no doubt feelings would evolve into the bedrock a marriage could depend upon. He would be a good and responsible father to this child, and when his own children came along…

Damn. He'd almost forgotten this afternoon's meeting to sort out his own will. Now making certain provisions seemed doubly important—provisions Tamara might not understand or like. But he couldn't let that sway him.

Cold drops splashed on their heads, as they stepped out of his vehicle.

When he circled her waist and swept her close, she laughed before her supple curves melded against him like hot wax molding to its cast. As she settled, the bow of her lips lifted so slightly, he wondered if he imagined her seductive smile.

Snaking her arms around his neck, she snuggled in. "Guess it's my lucky day."

His heart pounded. "Mine, too."

She stroked his Adam's apple with a knuckle. "We could make it even luckier?"

Primal heat surged through his veins. Eyes burning into hers, he set her palm against his cheek. "Are we talking satin sheets?"

"They don't have to be satin."

A fresh water smell rolled in from the east as Armand's heat combusted. Growling deep in his throat, he shifted her slightly to accommodate what felt like molten rock. "We'd decided to wait."

Hesitation flickered across her eyes before she threaded her fingers up the side of his neck, over his ear, through his hair. One shoulder lifted as her head angled up. For the first time her mouth sought out his, rather than the other way around.

She worked the kiss with an ease and sincerity that pumped his blood up past overload. Her perfume connected with the primitive part of his brain that reacted purely on instinct. His hand slid down her skirt, over the firm length of her thigh. He grinned at the mix of images…pure heaven and just as pure sin.

When she drew away, his essence went with her, like a thunder crack after lightning.

Her gaze followed the motion of her hand fanning over his chest. "Today made me realize again how fickle life can be. One minute you're here, sailing along, thinking you have nothing to worry about, then…bam! Everything collapses and you want back what you had before, and want it more than ever." Her eyes searched his. "I want you."

More droplets fell, catching and glistening on her lashes while her admission hung between them. The hope in her dilated eyes cried out for the obvious reply. Not I want you, but I love you. And he ought to say it, not only to cement the deal, so to speak, but also to make her happy. And he wanted that for reasons other than the satisfaction she gave him, and would give for years to come. She deserved to be loved.

Or, at least, believe that she was.

He was about to speak when the sprinkle turned into a stinging downpour. He found her free hand and, holding it tight raced with her beneath an archway dotted with climbing roses, two pairs of feet splashing madly toward the house. When they reached the back patio, Armand flicked his wet hands, swept open one half of the French doors and ushered her inside.

To save her worrying unnecessarily, Armand phoned Ruth when they'd got in the car. He shot a glance around for her now and noticed his favorite cheesecake sitting on the counter. An accompanying note told them to celebrate. He glanced over to Tamara, indicated the cake, and winked. "I love the way Ruth thinks."

She smiled even as a tremor wracked her body. The air-conditioning was on high to fight the prestorm humidity, and she was soaked through. Her sheer white dress clung like plastic wrap. Every line and curve and peak seemed to cry out for him to take immediate

action. She wanted him and—tradition be damned!—
he was going to take her.

He shook free of her spell long enough to fetch
towels from a nearby linen press. A moment later, her
shaking subsided as he dutifully rubbed her back, arms,
breasts.

As his actions gently rocked her, she hummed over
a grin. "I think it would be smarter to ditch the clothes."

His desire shot a level higher, harder. "When your
mind is made, you don't fool around, do you?"

"I'm only thinking of Ruth." She slid a sandaled toe
through the puddle at their feet, making a smiley-face
pattern. "We're dripping all over her clean floor."

"Maybe we should drip our way to the pool area."

"You promised me sheets."

He mock-frowned. "You were the one who suggested linen."

"And you gave me this ring, which means we're
supposed to be happy." She wove a finger around his
shirt buttons. "Make me happy."

He knew this Tamara had been hiding in there
somewhere. Mother of mercy, was he glad she'd
finally come out.

Bending, he swung her into his arms. His soggy
shoes squelched on the tiles as he strode toward the
stairs and her bedroom.

To the victor go the spoils.

Armand set her down at her bedroom doorway. Her
feet, minus the flat sandals, had barely sunk into the
downy snow-white carpet before he began to prowl,

crowding her back into the room. Tamara shuddered, not from cold but the intensity of the naked want smoldering in his eyes.

Moving ever nearer, he tore the shirttail out from his trousers and blindly undid his shirt. Mesmerized, she watched the deft action as he released the last button.

His chin jerked at her sodden dress. "Can I help?"

He peeled the shirt from each muscular arm with a roll of his shoulders. She sucked down a hot breath. Oh, Lord, her mouth felt like the Simpson Desert. "Maybe a glass of water."

"I thought we were celebrating. If you weren't pregnant, I'd suggest champagne…." Still prowling, he ripped off his belt and dropped it with as little ceremony as he had the shirt. "After we're done."

His olive skin was a masterpiece in polished muscle, from his hard-ridged stomach to twin rock pecs and shoulders that weren't so much large as formidable. His bulging biceps seemed to be on alert, his forearms powerful and corded with sinew. His sensuality was so vital, so real, she could literally taste it. Salty. Uncensored.

Her focus lifted to his face.

His eyes were dark, the bright irises drowned by desire. A wicked lopsided smile reached out to taunt her.

"Tamara," he admonished, "I hope you're not thinking of pulling out."

A fire ate up her legs as she backed up. A wet carpet of hair slapped her back as she shook her head a little too hard. "Nope. Not at all."

He chuckled. "Then stop running."

He stooped to flip off one shoe and the other. They

landed with a soft thump on the floor, more crumbs for the trail. Nerve endings catching light, she stopped to let him catch her. His heat struck her anew, searing like a blast of steam. He was right. She wanted this, had asked for it. She just hadn't expected to feel so…overwhelmed.

He seemed fascinated by the motion of his palm sculpting her shoulder. "Isn't that better?"

She leaned farther into his touch and felt immediately wrapped in a cocoon spun of competence and steel. "Much."

He found the zipper at her back. A moment later, the air brushed her damp skin. He slid the wet fabric from her shoulders and kissed the exposed curve of her neck. "Better still?"

Head back. Eyes closed. Tingling all over. "You can stop convincing me now."

"Not a chance."

The dress dropped heavily at her feet. The fiery tips of his hands edged in and around her panties' elastic, skimming her bottom. "You definitely need some help with these." One hand wove up, threading under her bra's back strap. "And this must be annoying. Feels wet right through." The ice-pink bra snapped undone.

Pangs of need curled in her stomach. Burying her nose in his chest, she breathed in the heady scent of prime male flesh. But clearly, he wanted her mouth where he could enjoy it. He cupped her face and kissed her deeply, maneuvering the bra 'til it fell. When her breasts brushed his abdomen, the longing was so intense she thought she might pass out.

He drew back and a line cut between his brows. "You're pale."

Her hands clenched his forearms. Yes, she was pregnant. However, "I don't need kid gloves." She pulled him close. "I need more of this."

Her mouth found his and his groan of appreciation vibrated through her fingertips.

"All the same," he murmured, half-kissing, half-talking, "I won't take chances."

She locked her arms around his waist, refusing to let him go. "Honestly. I'm fine."

He chuckled, a deep rich sexy sound. "Don't worry. I just need an excuse to carry you off to bed. I've been good long enough." His grin was crooked as he swept her up. "Can't tell you how much I've looked forward to being bad."

He crossed to the sumptuous lilac quilt. His gaze lingered on her lips before he did the most amazing thing. He swung her higher and set her to *stand* on the quilt.

Her stomach squeezed around excitement, shock and wide-eyed self-consciousness. She felt so vulnerable, parked there in front of him, every imperfection on display. Her hips were too wide, her legs, too skinny. Yet he looked her over as if every inch were perfection.

She partway covered her breasts, which felt suddenly twice as full and ten times more sensitive. "What are you doing?"

"Admiring the view." He took her hands away then brushed his lips near her navel. "You're beautiful. Don't hide it."

But she'd never done this before, made love with a man who affected her so deeply and on so many crazy, sublime, sometimes frustrating levels. The emotions were so strong, crashing over her, pinning her down and at the same time giving her wings. A month ago she couldn't have imagined trusting the cool, insistent man who hadn't let up and tracked her down. Remarkable, but now she couldn't see herself married to anyone else.

She'd discovered today she trusted Armand. But more than that…she was tumbling, head over heels in love with him. Surely tonight he would let her know he felt the same way.

Her heartbeat thudded madly in her chest, in her ears, as he clutched the triangle of fabric at her vee and dragged the silk down. Her eyes drifted shut as indescribable pleasure released a firestorm through her bloodstream.

He steadied her as she held onto his forearm and stepped from the last of her clothing. Cradling her bottom in his hot hands, he brought that newly exposed part of her close.

A breathtaking shudder claimed her as he kissed her *there,* so softly, it was nothing more than a touch. So tender, she thought she might weep.

His grip tightened. "You can't know how many times I've dreamed of making love with you."

The husky sincerity of his words stilled her. Smiling, she wound her fingers through his strong, black hair. "I wish I'd been there."

He chuckled, and Tamara dissolved more as his hands came around with an agonizing lack of speed. His fingers trailed up, then down her sides as his tongue twirled a lazy motion where her thigh met her most private parts. Her moan came from the very depths of her soul.

His thumbs winged down to massage her inner thighs as his mouth suctioned onto a quivering portion of flesh just above her bikini line. One fire-infused hand inched up her belly to find her breast, to roll and pull and adore its responsive tip.

Drifting in an ecstasy-induced haze, she understood the smile in his voice more than his words.

"This scene is a little uneven."

His weight shifted back.

Cast by the raging storm outside, a theater of rocking shadows inhabited the room. In the midst of those shadows stood Armand, an arsenal of sinew rippling as he worked to remove his trousers. Cement-hard pecs jostled as both shorts and pants came down to reveal powerful thighs and, when he straightened, a sight that took the rest of her breath away.

He had the physique of an athlete in his prime—every amazing inch, rock-solid and memorable. Her wandering gaze hooked onto his. He smiled as if he knew something she didn't.

"Ready?"

"Don't tease," she pleaded. "Not now." The antici-pation of twining her limbs with his, making love all the way, was close to killing her.

He moved forward, placed her arms around his neck and dropped moist, savoring kisses over her waist. Arrows of desire flew to her core when he reached the curve of her breast. The tip of his tongue trailed around the tender flesh, around and around, 'til she thought she might go mad. She hugged him in and he tasted her fully, sucking gently while his tongue still worked its magic.

His teeth grazed as he released her. Hands circling her waist, he lifted her off the bed and against him, letting her slide all the way 'til her toes touched the carpet.

The pad of one finger traced her temple, her cheek, finally skimming her parted mouth. He dipped to suckle her bottom lip as that fingertip fell to rim her other tight nipple.

Oh, Lord. Any second, she'd go up in flames.

He grabbed a fistful of quilt and flicked it back at the same moment a streak of lightning tore open the sky. A second later, an earth-shattering roll of thunder seemed to shake the room. She jumped, and Armand's shielding arms reassured her.

He bent to search her eyes. "It's only a storm."

She survived a test of fire today. Nothing could unravel her now, particularly not typical summer weather.

She thatched her fingers at the back of his neck and drew herself up toward him. "Just hurry up and kiss me again." She murmured against the yielding pressure of his lips, "Keep kissing me. Don't ever stop."

He hoisted her up and she stretched out on the smooth, cool sheets. The fresh laundered smell, hinting at lavender, surrounded her. Armand's lowering frame blocked what natural light still filtered in through the window. The whole world seemed suspended in shadow.

The mattress dipped as he edged in beside her. Over the sound of rain pelting against the window, their labored breathing joined. The heat of his body was molten. Like warmed butter, she melted against it.

His fingers trailed her tummy and lower, between her thighs. Wanting more, she angled toward him, bending her leg and raising that knee to rest over his hip. When he nudged closer—his mouth snatching kisses from her brow, his touch exploring—she felt swept away, a petal sucked along in the wake of a torrent.

Between their steaming bodies, the edge of his hand slid up to brush the tangible bud of her need. The jolt of pleasure made her jump even as a pressure, low and deep inside, began to burn and throb. Already almost flying, she arched more into the embrace.

She lost herself in sensation and building emotion that surpassed any joys she'd known before. This felt right…so incredibly, wonderfully right.

Her crescendo erupted. Her heart seemed to stop as her skin, this room, the universe, contracted. The walls inside her coiled exquisitely tight before the tension broke free to flash and pulse throughout her body.

As her world rocked on delicious tremors of release, he held her close, kissing her exactly the way she needed to be kissed. Finally, reluctantly, she drifted back, blood humming and heart full.

With great tenderness, he whispered, "How was Act One?"

Dreamy, she wiggled closer, reveling in the pleasure fizzes playing along every nerve ending. "How many acts are there?"

His damp chest inflated. "I wouldn't worry. It's going to be a very long season."

His palm came over to press her in and she sucked back a gulp of air as he entered her feminine core. An amazing heat sizzled through her. Her insides quivered and heartbeat went from impressive canter to furious gallop.

This was only the tip of him. Only the beginning.

He waited a few seconds then nuzzled into the hair near her ear. He nipped her earlobe then pushed a little deeper. A battalion of sparks zapped through her system. When he withdrew almost completely, instead of receding, those electric sensations imploded.

Her voice was a croak. "More."

She felt his strain. The trembling arm holding her was close to crushing. This time he moved slowly, more deeply, palm gliding down her outside thigh, ironing back up 'til he weighed her sensitive breast. His thumb brushed its tip at the same moment he immersed himself all the way. Her gasp sucked down to her toes.

Gradually her muscles relaxed to the point where he could move within her. His jaw flexed against her cheek. "Still with me?"

Her answer was a shivery sigh.

His rhythm increased, grinding her body close as she slipped against his muscular frame. The slow burn, low and pressing, grew more urgent. When he held her in a telltale bear hug, his heart might have burst through his chest, it pounded so savagely against her. A final squeeze, he shuddered, then sighed hard and long.

Tamara could barely catch her breath or wipe the contented smile from her face.

When she finally opened her eyes, the shadows had receded a little. A tree limb lashed against the huge arch window that presided over the room. Still floating, she surveyed the art on the wall—a couple of landscapes and one of a sad little boy. A group of crystal figures—unicorns, fairies and angels—sat quietly in their locked glass cabinet. This had been her bedroom these past weeks. Soon, perhaps as soon as tomorrow, the master suite would have a mistress.

Smiling, she nestled into what felt like an endless plateau of warm, bullet-proof steel. Her fingers ran over the field of hair that sprinkled his chest and arrowed silkily down to his belly—

He hiccupped out a short laugh and snatched her hand.

She frowned, blinked, then smiled. "My God, you're ticklish."

He cleared his throat, but didn't release her hand. "Only in that one specific, rarely noticed spot."

"You don't look like the ticklish kind."

"What kind would that be?"

She tossed it up. "Not like you."

"You mean surly. Focused. Determined."

"Alpha. Built. Sexy."

He cradled her closer and she burrowed in, fingers splayed over his chest. An impulse grabbed her. She let her fingers walk a few inches.

His hand captured hers. "Stop right there. A man has to have some secrets."

She put on a pout. "Things he won't even share with his wife?"

"Believe me, some things are best left private."

She grinned. "You think?"

"There's nothing you'd like to keep buried?"

Tamara noticed his tone change. Her thoughts skipped, and her mood dipped.

Best left private…left buried. She thought back to her conversation with Ruth. After hearing the full story today, she understood far more. She felt so sorry for both those boys. Sorry for the whole sordid mess. But what mattered now was them being together, being a couple. And, beyond all else, the baby being safe.

She breathed in Armand's sensual male scent and whispered into the quiet, "Thank you for being there today."

He sounded almost surprised. "I wanted to be. It was my place."

Her heart doubled size. Surely Marc would rest easy if he could hear that. But now, lying naked in Armand's arms, wasn't the time for that kind of memory.

Her thoughts wandered off toward the future. Christmases, birthdays, school…

Suddenly animated, she pushed up onto one elbow. "Do you like baseball?"

He grinned. "Sure."

"How about football?"

"Aren't too many men who don't. Why?"

She glowed looking at the vision in her mind. "Saturday mornings at footy practice."

"We're not certain he's a boy, remember."

"Girls play football, too," she reminded him, then

had another thought. "What age do you think you'll in-troduce him—or her—to De Luca Enterprises?" She laughed. "I can picture a toddler in a necktie sitting behind a giant U-shaped desk."

Armand's smile was thin. "That's a long way off."

"Which part? The toddler or running the company?"

"She might not have a good business head?"

Tamara flinched. *Like I don't have a good business head?*

But another connection bothered her more. "Am I missing something? You're so driven and focused on DLE, and on tradition and heritage…I thought you'd be teaching him about stock market surges before Kinder-garten, and 'Crush all opposition 101' by third grade."

Any remains of a smile drained from his eyes. "You should stop studying my father's portrait. You're getting us confused."

A withering feeling fell through her. From all accounts, Dante had been relentless, both in his business and private life. No doubt Armand's childhood had been dominated by rigorous training designed to prepare for his inheritance. Unlike his father, Armand had inferred he would not repeat that mistake. She would be forever thankful for it.

She touched his hand. "Sorry. I didn't mean to imply that you were a…" She searched for a word other than tyrant.

He dropped a quick kiss on her brow, then flung the sheets off and pushed to his feet. That withering feeling fell through her again, faster this time. Her fingers curled into the sheets. "Where are you going?"

"Hate to cut this short, but I have a meeting."

Now? She sat bolt upright and the sheet pooled around her waist.

His gaze fell to her breasts. Jaw flinching, he collected his trousers. "I'd like to stay, Tamara, but this meeting is important. I can't delay it."

She slid the covering up over her cooling body. "I didn't mean to…"

The words trailed off again. He was a busy man. But she could take heart knowing that when they truly needed him, she and the baby would come first. A baby who would grow to help run DLE, a multimillion-dollar company that controlled so much and so many. The concept was so incredible she could barely get her head around it.

She watched him sweep his shirt off the floor. "When will you be home?"

"Not sure."

Finding a grin, she brought up her knees and hugged them tight. "Will we mess up my bed some more or try yours out?"

His arms shot through his sleeves. He studied the crumpled fabric and, frowning, ripped the shirt off again. "Actually, I think it's a good idea if we hold off now until the wedding."

Tamara's jaw dropped. Her mouth refused to work. She could form only one word. "Why?"

Expression torn, or maybe just a touch irritated, he crossed over to her. "I'm not sorry this happened. But don't you want our wedding night to be special?"

He was fine with abstaining while she was already

aching for him again? Tears pricked the back of her eyes and her cheeks grew hot. "Be truthful. Is it the tradition thing?" Her vision blurred. "Or just me?"

He sat down and curled a finger around her cheek. "Without a word of a lie, you were better than wonderful. But our next time together will be as man and wife. We'll share ourselves intimately, completely, and seal the commitment we make on that day."

Her mouth twisted on a wry smile. "Are you worried I won't marry you if we 'share' too much beforehand?"

God help her, the wounded part of her meant it. Maybe he considered his decision a romantic gesture, but their falling into bed couldn't be undone. In her humble opinion, it was a bit late to lose sleep over traditional values now.

His gaze sharpened and he stood to his full imposing height. "I'm late." He moved to swoop up his belt, paused, and came back. He tipped her head up for a parting kiss, but for the first time in what seemed like forever the embrace didn't leave her wistful, so much as wondering.

He looked at her for a long, heart-swelling moment then walked away.

She called out, "Will I organize dinner? Maybe we could go out." He might be leaving on a down note, but they still had today's medical reprieve to celebrate.

He hesitated at the door. His hand on the jamb, he flicked an apologetic look over his shoulder. "No promises, but I'll try."

Sinking into the pillow, she told herself to focus on the positives. She and Armand were one hundred percent compatible in the bedroom and in a few short days the unimaginable would happen.

She would become Mrs. Armand De Luca and, soon after, their baby would be born. Surely no one could ask for more.

CHAPTER NINE

Armand's heart swelled with pride watching his bride of two hours mingle with the crowd gathered for their Christmas Eve wedding reception.

He'd been told by the bride herself that she wore an empire-style gown. The beads bordering the modestly cut halter-top were crystal and the fabric felt like the world's softest petals. The image of Tamara from earlier would live in his memory forever. She'd moved like some divine vision down the botanic garden path toward the gazebo where he'd waited, veil a gauzy river that trailed behind her for what had seemed like miles.

That veil was wrapped around her arm now as she stopped to chat with an inquisitive pair—a rowing buddy and his very pregnant wife. Tamara tipped her head and the diamond tiara, set upon her crown of sable hair, flashed in the golden light. Armand smiled at the sound of her tinkling laughter. Sipping champagne, he surveyed the extent of the extravagant ballroom, which provided a magnificent wall-to-wall view of the harbor's starlit waters.

Approximately eighty guests were in attendance, a

smallish gathering by anyone's standards. But given the time frame, it had been easy enough, and he'd been happy to comply with her wish to keep the numbers down. Despite tabloid reports, he didn't thrive on "society," simply knew how to play the game when need be.

They caught each other's eye and Tamara's heart-shaped face shone. When she raised her flute, filled with a nonalcoholic variety of bubbly, a pang of guilt curled low in his gut.

He recognized the look of a beautiful young lady in love, he only wished he could return that depth of feeling. Of course, he cared for Tamara. So much, it sometimes frightened him.

He must maintain control. No matter how tempting, he would never again surrender to a force that could lift him as high as the heavens, only to crash again. That didn't mean he couldn't give her the fairy tale she wanted and deserved. He doubted he'd have any trouble pretending to have lost his heart for love of her. He'd come close to losing his mind with *want*. Tonight, at last, he would enjoy some relief.

She begged off from her present company and, collecting one corner of her satin gown, headed toward him. On the way, she grabbed the arm of an older woman, who seemed to be enjoying herself watching couples slow-dancing to the mellow music of an eight-piece band.

Armand blindly checked his black bow tie and put on his most charming smile. He took Elaine Kendle's hand in greeting before gathering his wife near.

Tamara's scent was similar to the roses sitting tall in the glass vases set upon round tables dressed in gold, white and a soft pink.

He stole a kiss, lingering close to murmur, "You're beautiful."

While Tamara's cheeks turned the color of ripe cherries, Elaine audibly sighed. "Always was. Doubt you could've got anyone prettier than Tammy." She settled a worn hand on her daughter's tulle-wrapped arm, pale green eyes glistening. "I'm just so glad everything worked out."

Tamara hesitated a beat before her expression melted and she came forward to kiss her mother's lined cheek. "I'm glad you're here."

The undertone was clear: she hadn't been certain Elaine would come. It would remain his and Elaine's secret that, to make it easier, he had paid her plane fare and added a decent amount for an outfit and associated needs. Overnight accommodation in this inner-city hotel was available, too, as was the case for all their guests, though he couldn't anticipate numbers. Many had young families they wished to wake up with tomorrow morning. Next year, he and Tamara would be in the same boat.

Elaine stepped back, cloaking her emotion by smoothing a hand down the front of her peach-colored skirt suit. "Are you still studying, Tammy? Must almost be done by now."

Tamara blinked as if surprised—and delighted— Elaine had remembered. "I have an exam in a month's time. Then two more subjects before I get my degree."

"It was something you'd set your heart on." Elaine's

smile came slowly. "I'm proud you're finishing when other girls might've lost heart."

An awkward pause followed and Armand knew the two women were considering the contrast in their lives. One had barely gotten by because she'd chosen to settle for her lot; the other recently lost everything, but still retained the spirit to achieve—the defining quality of a winner.

Not that Tamara would ever need to use that degree. Once the baby came along, then the next, she'd have her hands full. She wouldn't want to waste her energies worrying about restarting a business. He respected her ideals as well as the valid reasons she'd strived so hard to attain her independence. But her life was different now and given time he was certain she would come to understand that working outside of the home could spoil a happy family life. No one wanted that.

Elaine sipped her champagne over a grin. "I've finished a course, myself."

"You're studying?"

"As of last week, it's official. I didn't want to say anything 'til I was certain. I'm an authorized wedding celebrant." She glanced around. "A bit of coincidence, wouldn't you say?"

Tamara squeaked and flung an arm around her mother. Armand heard her throaty murmur over the animated chatter and occasional *ting* of crystal glasses. "My turn to say I'm proud. I can't tell you how much."

Eyes glistening again, Elaine patted Tamara's back then gradually pulled away. "It took me a long time to learn a big lesson. Everyone has choices," she explained with a simple shrug. "But you always knew that, didn't you, Tammy? And you've made the very best choice today. A promise that you'll keep for the rest of your lives." She leaned into Armand and growled. "Don't you dare let her go."

He grinned. "Believe me, I won't."

Happy with that, Elaine exhaled and cast a glance over to the buffet. "Think I'll grab some of that delicious-looking dessert. Don't know I've ever heard of a wedding 'cheesecake' before."

As she left, Armand qualified, "Only the top layer, which, I think, is a crying shame. In my opinion, fruit cake is overrated."

Tamara laughed and he angled around to hold her hand in his. He spoke to her eyes, reassuring her. "She seems nice."

With a slight shake of her head, Tamara sighed. "I guess she always was. It was just hard to grab a moment when she was home, happy and not catching up on sleep."

"A marriage celebrant." He grinned. "Seems like the bad times are well and truly behind her." He would look after Elaine's needs in any case; Tamara's family was now his.

He lifted and rocked her hand from side to side, admiring the ruby and simple gold band, which would forever symbolize the vows they'd made today, but admiring the sense of connection and belonging far more.

Like Tamara, he'd missed out on a family growing up. After his farce of an engagement to Christine Sawyer, he'd pushed aside a goal that had quietly gnawed at him for years. He would never enjoy a friendship shared between close brothers, though he understood in part "Marc Earle's" reasons for renouncing his birth name and, later, Armand's offer of a share in the company. Good chance Armand would have done the same if his father had disowned him. Still, he couldn't deny that tonight he felt a sense of justice: the wheel had turned full circle.

He frowned. He could do nothing about Marco; Angela's fair-haired boy was gone. But today the "dark prince" had reclaimed what he'd lost so long ago—a family. He had a wife whom he would keep close and cherish, and a child who would take his ordained place within the De Luca matrix and, subsequently, inherit. Not as much as his own children when they came along, of course.

He winced a little. But, when all was said and done, the share he had in mind was certainly a more than adequate cut. When the time came, Tamara would understand. Naturally children from their marriage, sons he had spawned, would receive a greater share. That's just the way the world worked, the way things had to be. This child would still be provided for, the way Marco would have done.

He lowered her hand. "Did you tell your mother about the baby?"

She glanced at Elaine, who was speaking with an interested gentleman, their silver forks poised over plates of chocolate cheesecake. "I thought I'd keep that surprise for another day—" her eyes narrowed "—but I have a sneaking suspicion she already knows."

Glass in hand, his knuckle grazed her cheek. "Perhaps because you're glowing."

She blushed. "All brides are supposed to be radiant."

"Not like you." He edged nearer so the hand he held pressed low against his jacket. "I'm catching light just touching you. Imagine an hour from now." If he wasn't careful, he'd self-combust.

Her expression sobered. "After that afternoon we spent together, I was upset when you suggested we wait." Her lashes lowered. "But now I'm glad we did."

Certain no one would mind, he captured a lingering kiss from his bride. God, but she tasted sweet.

He exhaled on a grin. "You're going to tire of me hauling you back to the bedroom during our honeymoon." And all the days and months and years beyond that.

"Phuket has lovely beaches. I'm sure I won't mind sand instead of sheets occasionally."

Her seductive smile did more than warm him. He filled his lungs imagining the scents and sounds of the Thailand paradise. "Moonlight shimmering over water, palm fronds gently swaying. I can picture it now."

She slanted her head. "It is hot?"

"Very," he replied.

"Can you picture me?"

"More clearly than anything."

"What am I wearing?"

He drank in her lips. "Aside from the flower in your hair, what do you think?"

"Armand, what a splendid evening!"

Armand's nostrils flared and his backbone stiffened as Matthew Mohill's regal frame stalked out from behind a group of guests. On his tuxedoed arm hung a demure-looking blonde.

Cornered, and not happy about it, Armand filed thoughts of Phuket aside to take care of pleasantries. "May I present my wife, Tamara."

Matthew's smile might have been genuine. "It's delightful to meet you." On taking her hand, he noticed the ruby and his high forehead crept back more. "Armand…" He coughed out a humorless laugh. "I'm a little surprised. This ring doesn't have fond memories for you."

Heat accumulated around Armand's collar. Had he once thought this man a friend? His words barely made it past his teeth. "Now it does."

"Armand explained its past." Tamara beamed into her new husband's eyes. "I fell in love with the ruby at first sight."

Matthew seemed to chew on that before he pivoted toward his own companion. "I don't believe either of you know my bride."

Eager little Evie stepped forward. "Such a beautiful ceremony! What a gorgeous backdrop, with all those summer flowers and the perfect weather. I'm so glad it wasn't too hot. And releasing butterflies from those Renaissance urns at the end…" Evie emitted a long dreamy sigh.

Smiling, Tamara tipped her head. "I thought it was a nice touch."

Evie blinked. "You thought of that?"

Armand took the opportunity to brag on his wife's behalf. "Tamara organized everything, including a fireworks display scheduled as a finale tonight."

Evie giggled. "Sounds like you have a knack, Tamara. Maybe you should start a business." Though he flinched, Armand was certain no malice was intended.

Evie looked at Matthew with the same adoration Armand had seen in Tamara's eyes a moment ago. "Our wedding was beautiful, too, wasn't it, darling? On the beach, orchard leis around our necks. You looked so handsome."

Armand lifted a brow. That affection wasn't manufactured. And for the life of him, he couldn't see this woman goading Matthew into unsheathing his corporate sword. She looked more like a dove than a war hawk. Dammit all, if things were different, he could share in their happiness rather than plot against it, or, more specifically, Matthew's attempt to seize control of DLE.

"We have some news," Matthew said, returning his attention to the newly married couple. "You're the first to know. We're expecting."

Armand's grip on his glass, and Tamara's waist, tightened. "Expecting what?"

Matthew chuckled. "A baby, Armand! A child. Maybe two."

Evie's mahogany-colored eyes gleamed. "Twins run in my family. We'd love a boy and girl straight off. We've already chosen names."

The room was spinning…chandeliers, waiters…but all Armand could see was Matthew's thin top lip sweeping into a "beat-cha" grin.

Tamara performed a duty of which Armand, at the moment, was incapable. She came forward and hugged

Matthew's young wife. "I'm so happy for you." Her voice rang with honesty. Evie was someone you just had to like. "When are you due?"

Evie looped her arm through Matthew's. "I'm fourteen, almost fifteen weeks."

Tamara gasped. "Really!"

Armand's squeezed Tamara's arm to silence her. Their baby was the same gestational age. It might be wise to keep your enemies close. It was also wise to keep the best up your sleeve for the surprise attack.

He knew what Matthew had planned. 9:00 a.m. on Armand's birthday, he would lodge the necessary paperwork to finalize that explicit term in Dante's will—no De Luca child and that margin of controlling interest would remain with the trustee, should the trustee so deem.

The ironic thing was Dante had trusted Matthew, as a man would trust his own brother to do right by his son. That clause had been nothing more than a solid nudge for Armand to marry and ensure DLE remained, largely, a family concern. Dante would never have believed Matthew would take advantage of the situation and convince himself he was entitled to more than his share.

Matthew spoke directly to Armand, his ice-blue gaze challenging. "We were speaking with Riley Peters and Jack Gibson. Fellow board members," he explained to Tamara. "They were remarking on how well we went last set of figures."

Armand sent what might be interpreted as an easy smile. "Good to hear there's no complaints over how the company's run."

Matthew pulled a pained faced. "I did hear unhappy rumblings about the expansion issue."

Armand drew a knife. "Hear, or instigate?"

Matthew pretended offence. "Just passing it on, son."

Armand was about to demand Matthew back away from calling him "son," but he'd been reeled in far enough. His wedding reception was not the place for a showdown. He respected his wife's feelings too much for that.

Beside him, Tamara gave her apologies. "Would you excuse me? A couple of friends are frantically waving me over. I haven't caught up with them yet. Kristin and Melanie," she said to Armand and he nodded. Tamara took Evie's hand. "Best wishes for the baby. It's an exciting time."

Matthew affected a bow as Tamara moved off. "I was going to mingle more myself after mentioning that Barclays had done well, too."

Armand dropped his glass. It bounced, then broke on the carpet while Tamara froze midstep. Frown quizzical, she turned slowly back.

A waiter rushed over, wiping the drink spilt over Armand's shoes. Evie stepped back, a protective hand on her tummy while Matthew brushed his lapel.

"What did you say?"

Matthew met Tamara's perplexed gaze in a way that suggested he hadn't heard properly. He'd heard her just fine. Matthew had set him up. He should have anticipated something like this. Matthew had delved into his bride's past, hoping to stir and fling some mud. He knew Barclays was the company that neglected to pay Tamara's business invoice months ago.

What else did Matthew know?

The older man edged around to Tamara. "I mentioned Barclays have done extremely well. They're a big hardware chain." Naive Evie nodded, as if that explained it all. "Have you taken some interest in DLE's subsidiaries, my dear?"

Tamara blindly set her flute on a passing waiter's tray. Her face was ashen, dazed. "Barclays..." She looked to Armand and questioned, pleaded, with those big green eyes. He held the cool column of her arm and shot Matthew a glare meant not to harm but annihilate.

While Matthew merely raised a brow, Armand gathered unbelievable control to address his wife. "Nice meeting you, Evie."

He moved Tamara off to a relatively quiet corner of the room, a semicircle alcove with wedding gifts stacked high to toppling on a table.

Her words were threadbare. "Matthew said Barclays is a subsidiary of DLE." Her short laugh held a hysterical note. "He's wrong." Her brows opened up. "Isn't he?"

"This isn't the time. We'll discuss it later." He gripped her forearms. "I just need to reassure you—"

"You knew, didn't you?"

Her voice was a flat line. Her eyes were devoid of light. The almighty knot in Armand's gut pulled and twisted 'til he groaned. "I didn't know...not at first."

Tamara slumped as if a bullet had struck her chest. "You knew and didn't tell me?"

"It's not that simple."

The pain in her eyes hardened. "You can say that again."

A high-pitched female voice flew over their heads, rebounding off the curved wall making it sound ten times more invasive. "Tamara! Oh, my God, you look like a fairy tale princess."

Heartbeat running amok, Armand stepped aside as either Kristin or Melanie hugged Tamara, who responded with the vibrancy of a rag doll. Then the next twin had her squeeze.

One of them held out her hand for Armand to accept. "I'm Kristin." She indicated the other. "My sister, Melanie. We just want to say how totally thrilled we are for our friend. Absolutely no one deserves happiness more."

He pinned on an appropriate smile. "Thank you for coming. We appreciate you both sharing our day."

They chatted for a couple of minutes. Tamara seemed subdued but at least partway recovered by the time Armand bowed off to track Matthew down. Wedding reception or not, there was going to be a one helluva showdown.

His gaze swept the buzzing room like a laser beam. Matthew was not only shrewd, he was smart. He was gone, leaving Armand to clean up the mother of all messes.

CHAPTER TEN

STANDING on the balcony, Tamara gazed over the night's shimmering silk harbor then, fighting down a shiver, hugged herself. The air was sultry—typical "Down Under" Christmastime weather. The slight breeze, drifting in off the water, certainly wasn't the reason she was trembling, even given her minimal clothing.

She'd left her wedding reception forty minutes ago. Had come directly to the bridal suite, slipped off her dress and drowned herself beneath a shower's cold stinging spray. The water hadn't washed away the humiliation. How could Armand have kept that information from her?

She was concentrating on the tiniest, loneliest-looking star in the velvet night sky when the suite's door swooshed open. Pulse rate spiking, Tamara held her breath and listened to it click shut. Imagining her disgruntled husband moving through the expansive, plush room, she closed her eyes and waited. She was the one, not Armand, who should be upset. In fact, she was visibly shaking.

Although she stood with her back to the room, she

sensed his overwhelming presence when he stopped to fill the doorway. Heartbeat jackhammering in her throat, she calmly turned, swaddling a matching light wrap more securely around the negligee she'd taken such care to choose last week.

Armand seemed unaware of her ivory-colored chiffon. His chest, beneath the white dress shirt, rose and fell with deep but even breathing while his intense gaze pierced and challenged hers. His normally ordered hair was mussed, jacket open, black tie undone and hanging. He'd never looked more untamed or more handsome.

His hand flexed at his side before he joined her by the railing. His voice was deep, strained, almost threatening. "You left without telling me."

Her stomach muscles tugged, but she tried to ignore his raw sexuality and how much it affected her. "I made it 'til halfway through the fireworks display." Her chin kicked up. "I think I should be congratulated."

His frown hinted at disgust. "You make our wedding sound like a death sentence."

"I certainly hope not."

After a tense moment, he exhaled and rushed a hand through his hair. "I was held up with Mr. Zheng, the Chinese businessman I introduced you to."

Tamara nodded. Armand had sent an invitation when he'd learnt that Mr. Zheng would be in Australia at the time of their wedding.

Armand seemed to struggle for a moment. "I tried to get away…I wanted to leave…" He fell back against the railing. "I couldn't afford to offend him."

Right now, she wasn't interested in business associates, and neither should he be. Arms firmly crossed beneath her negligee's lace bodice, she picked up where they'd left off before Kristin and Melanie had interrupted.

"Why the hell didn't you tell me DLE owned Barclays?"

Pulse leaping in his jaw, he cast a glance out over Sydney's glittering cityscape. "Tamara, it's no secret we own a sizeable piece of that hardware chain. DLE has a stake in dozens of companies." He met her eyes. "What I didn't know was Barclays was the company that refused to pay your invoice."

Her fingers dug into their opposite arms as she mulled it over. His gaze was direct, open.

She let out a breath. Okay, so he hadn't known about the connection between his subsidiary's wrongdoings and her business's downfall when they'd met. But he damn well should have told her when he'd discovered the truth. "When did you find out?"

His arms spread out to brace his weight against the rail. "Same day I discovered Matthew's turnaround. I thought about telling you, but you were hovering on a ledge, deciding which way to jump. I thought you'd leap to conclusions. Take it the wrong way."

Perhaps sensing a slight retreat in her frosty attitude, he tipped forward.

She moved back. "Didn't you stop to think I might take it an even worse way when I did find out?"

The threat of tears prickled behind her eyes. She dropped her arms and bunched her hands, determined not to give in to emotion and cry. But she couldn't stop her throat and face from flaming when she recalled Matthew Mohill's triumphant gleam from those arctic-blue eyes. Armand was right. Any friendship they'd known before had been left behind by Matthew's lunge to attain ultimate control.

How ridiculous. A lifelong friendship wasted for the sake of money when both Armand and Matthew already had plenty. Did men of power put any limit on the sacrifices they would make in order to succeed? How absurd that Matthew should value material gain more highly than what he'd freely tossed away. He'd resort to anything to help weaken Armand's position, including detonating a bomb at his new rival's wedding.

She swallowed against the lump forming in her throat. "Do you have any idea what it was like for me to discover my husband of hours, the man I trusted, had deceived me?"

He'd moved closer again without her noticing. One dark brow arched and his gaze dipped. "Is that negligee supposed to be a hint?"

She dammed a rush of warmth at his approving gaze and swept her wrap closer. "Don't change the subject."

His head cocked. "I didn't think of it as deception." His hand stole out and fingers toyed with hers. "I didn't want to lose you."

One of the splinters of hurt wedged beneath her ribs dissolved, but others remained. She'd wanted today to be perfect and the evening to be a night she would never forget. She'd daydreamed constantly about lying with Armand again, of experiencing the heady thrill of his mouth on her body, his hands coaxing her to amazing places she needed to visit again and again. Yet here they were, arguing.

The alternative was to forgive him, try to understand, but she wasn't certain she could do that yet. Was this the kind of compromise she'd be expected to make from now on? "Marriage is supposed to be about making choices together. Respect, you said. Honesty. Those were the traditional values you wanted to uphold." Her vision misted. "Didn't you believe in the promises we made today?"

She had, with all her heart. When he'd recited those lines and she'd replied with her own, she had barely been able to speak for welling emotion—not from worry over making the wrong decision, but from certainty what she was doing was right. Her greatest wish had come true. She loved Armand as a wife should love a husband, with everything in her heart. But she'd given it all only to discover he'd held back.

His fingers twined around her hand as his eyes burned into hers. "Of course I believe in our vows. I only wanted to save you from any more pain."

His thumb rubbed her wrist and the battle raging inside of her dropped a grade.

He understood, didn't he? She didn't want to be patronized. She wanted to be loved. But perhaps even more, she wanted to count—to be seen and heard. She wasn't invisible. Never would be again.

He took her other hand and the tension locking her muscles eased another notch. She searched his eyes. "I lost my house over that incident."

His smile was supportive but also lopsided and sexy. "I'll buy you a château in the south of France."

She sighed heavily. "I don't want a château."

Still holding her hands, he gently twirled her under one arm in a dance move so he stood behind her, his arms wrapped around her waist. His graveled murmur brushed the sensitive shell of her ear. "The Barclays accountant was an imbecile. He's gone." His lips grazed her lobe. "If it makes any difference, yesterday I refunded the money owed to you as a bonus to your first week's allowance."

A shudder tripped up her spine. She tried to turn to face him, but his arms held and locked her in place. Her mouth tugged to one side. "Allowance. That makes it sound as if I'm being kept."

"You're my wife." His chin gently scraped her cheek. "Did you think I wouldn't look after you?" His mouth pressed against her temple and her insides began to glow and beat. "You know how much I care about you and the baby, don't you?"

His crisscrossed hands slid apart, over her stomach and higher to cup her shoulders. Her head lolled back, eyes drifted shut and breasts tingled for his touch. She thought of the incident at Dr. Fielding's and nodded. "Yes. I know."

He cared, but did he love them—love her—the way she'd come to love him? Over these past weeks her feelings had climbed until she'd reached this summit. Perhaps that's why his withholding something so important had hurt so much. She had truly expected the fairy tale ending. She thought he'd come to want that, too. He'd said as much before.

His palm dropped off her shoulder, taking both her wrap's sleeve and negligee's shoestring strap along with it. His mouth lowered to taste the spot. "Let's not quarrel. Don't you want to enjoy our wedding night?"

Of course she did. And with his mouth tracking the curve of her throat, his heat soaking into her back, it seemed impossible to verbally or physically deny.

She'd been justifiably upset. He was sorry he'd hurt her. He wouldn't do it again. Any moment he would confess that he loved her. She felt that as surely as the undeniable desire sizzling through her veins.

He eased the other sleeve and strap down. When she turned for him to embrace her, with his arms then his lips, her wrap and negligee slipped to the floor. As they came together, she fell into the sensation, giving herself over to the physical, lost in the wonder of how his body pressed a perfect fit into hers. The surge of her arousal, of his, obliterated any remaining doubt.

She belonged here, with him. Despite what had happened tonight, she'd never been more certain of anything.

Eyes closed, she frowned when his arms left her. Hearing the rustle of fabric, she grinned against his lips and understood. Blindly reaching out, she helped maneuver his jacket off the ledge of his shoulders. Next, two pairs of hands tumbled over one another to get to his shirt buttons. Not until she heard the zip of his trousers did she stop to think. A second later, a thunderbolt of alarm zapped through her.

Pulling away, she covered her breasts and darted a look around. "We're out in the open."

His smile passionate and ruthless, he dragged her close again. "On the penthouse floor of one of the highest buildings in Sydney in the middle of the night."

His palm glided down her stomach into the front of her panties. She gasped at the flash of heat, but shimmied back. "People still might see."

"I like fresh air."

He reached again, but she held up a hand. "I like privacy."

His growl was playful but determined. Grabbing her hand, he tugged her to the other door, which led to their bridal bedroom—large, fragrant and dressed all in snow-white. Once inside, he drew her gently in again. One hand on the dip of her naked back, the other holding her palm against his cheek, he began to move to imaginary music, swaying from side to side, then slowly around.

Her hand kneaded the polished, hard surface of his shoulder while her breasts grazed the sculptured form of his ribs. When the friction building below felt bright enough to see, she squeezed her muscles around a luscious coil of longing and tilted back her head. A silver moonbeam touched the lick of black hair fallen over his widow's peak while his eyes glistened with undiluted desire.

His deep husky voice seduced her all the more. "I didn't want to miss out on the last dance of the evening."

She imagined their guests gazing on now and shook her head, grinning. "We're not really dressed for it."

"You are so right."

After leading her backward, he hitched her up so she

landed just shy of the middle of the sumptuous king-sized bed. The fire curling through her blood roared louder when, one knee on the mattress, he leaned closer to ease the panties from her behind, then down her elevated legs.

His broad chest inflated. "Much better."

He removed the rest of his clothing then joined her on the bed. His hand slid up her side before he winged her shoulder in and his mouth dropped over hers.

Her outside leg craned up, her knee skimming back and forth just south of his hip. Hot sparks shot over her skin, igniting every inch while their tongues danced and hunger grew. After needing his love so desperately, at long last she felt released.

His hand grazed down to her waist, over her hip then across to her apex, which cried out for his touch.

He nipped her lower lip. "You feel like heaven."

She hummed in her throat and held his hand in place. "You, too." Silken, dreamy, delicious bliss.

He shifted, taking the peak of her breast in his mouth, playing with its bead while he continued to explore her. When his finger slid into her private warmth, she tensed for a giddy moment then melted on a sigh. The deep pulsing at her core was so intense, the energy made her shrink and grow with every beat. Sucking down a lungful of air, she gripped his ears and hauled him back up.

"Kiss me."

Their mouths joined at the same time he tipped her flat on her back. His palm gently kneaded her belly before a fingertip wove higher, tracing back and forth over the pattern of her ribs. The hot length of his shaft ground against her thigh as he shifted slightly to deepen the kiss. When he rediscovered her breasts, so full and aching with want, her need took a sweeping turn and landed her smack-bang in the middle of ecstasy.

I love you.

The words echoed through her mind, growing louder, sweeter, with every stroke and caress. Why didn't he say it? Now was the time…the first time of so many.

She held him tighter, her hands sliding over the domed length of his back, slick with perspiration. As if she'd given a sign, in one skillful movement he lay positioned on top. Acting on instinct, she threw her legs around his hips and thrust up while her head arced slowly back. She felt him looking down at her, studying her throat and lips before his thighs tensed and he eased into her.

Ripples of heat swam out from her center, building as they traveled to rock her from head to tingling foot. The butt of her hands dug like anchors into his sides as she drove her hips up then gyrated gently around.

He pumped slowly, snatching one, two, three kisses from her parted lips. "I didn't think it was possible," he murmured close to her mouth, "but you feel better than the first time."

She closed her eyes and reveled in his words. "I don't ever want to wait for you again."

If she never left his arms, she couldn't be happier.

A stronger breeze blew through the open door. As the sheer curtain flew and cooler air rushed in, their rhythm increased, becoming deeper, more urgent, his length hitting time and again a sensitive recess inside that throbbed like unstable TNT.

When he drove in to the hilt, her hands fell to grip the sheet at either side. Her inner walls hummed and squeezed before the fireball combusted, shooting whirling flames like a spinning wheel to every receptor of her body. On another plane, she felt tremors grip his frame at the same time his biceps bunched and pinioned her arms. The intense pleasure consuming her mind, body and soul flared and ebbed in delicious waves until the fire slowly died. Spent, he groaned as his dark head lowered to bury in her hair.

She felt both heavy and floating, alive yet stripped of every conceivable ounce of energy. Sighing over a contended smile, she maneuvered one arm out to run her fingers through his hair. He groaned again and nuzzled deeper toward her ear and neck, murmuring her name, filling her with indescribable warmth and newfound peace.

As the seconds ticked by, her euphoria subsided. She blinked into the darkened room, waiting for something else. Waiting for more words. Finally he shifted, and her blood began to wildly pump again. Brows slightly drawn, he searched her eyes, her face, then gathered her against his broad hard chest, his hand holding hers on his stomach. But while the silence should have been comfortable and the steady thumping of his heart should have completed her fulfillment, her cheeks began to burn.

He wasn't going to say it.

CHAPTER ELEVEN

ARMAND pulled up unexpectedly at the nursery doorway. His wife of two weeks stood in the center of the room, serenely gazing down at the cradle.

Back only a couple of days from their all too brief honeymoon, it had been one hell of a morning. An early start to the weekend seemed like a damn fine idea. He thought he might find Tamara in the garden and was on his way to the bedroom to change, jacket already ditched, when he'd happened upon her here.

Dressed in a soft yellow shift, she seemed absorbed in the motion of her hand running down the cradle's net. Her stream of sable hair lay draped over one shoulder. In profile, a wistful smile touched her lips.

Each time he laid eyes on her, the same urge struck. He needed to feel her, smell her, kiss her. No exception now. In fact, it grew stronger every day.

Heartbeat beginning to pound, he walked up behind and gently squeezed her shoulder. She spun around as if the devil had leapt down her throat.

Her hand flew to her chest and she gasped before her

wide eyes blinked in recognition. "Armand...you scared me half to death!"

Damn. He'd meant to surprise her, not frighten her. After enfolding her in his arms, he sampled those honeyed lips. "Forgive me?"

She let go a breath and surrendered a smile. "Well, just this once." She frowned and grabbed his wrist to check the time. "You're home early."

"I needed to see my wife." Game, set, match—it was official. He was addicted.

She wrapped her arms around his neck and swayed against him. "That's the nicest news I've had all week."

He searched her eyes, saw their hope and trust, and suppressed a stab of guilt. Instead he peered down, focusing on the bump settled between them. "How's baby?"

Her face glowed. "He was moving again."

She took his hand and pressed it to her tummy. He waited, concentrated, shifted his angle, then shook his head. "Can't feel a thing."

"It's like a tiny fish swimming around."

His hand dropped away. "Sounds strange."

"Feels wonderful." Both her hands cradled her belly. "Sometimes I want to pinch myself. Three months ago I didn't know where to turn, my life was in chaos." She shrugged. "Now I'm happily married."

He felt the yawning gap again. The one that needed to be filled with his confession of love. He wanted to. No reason he shouldn't be able to say it. They were only words. And the longer he didn't, the more he saw it in her eyes—the little question marks that hadn't quite disappeared since their wedding night.

The tension bracing his shoulders eased slightly when she broke their gaze and moved to the dollhouse in the far corner.

"So, what happened today? Any news on China?"

He slipped his hands into his trouser pockets. "Spoke with Mr. Zheng. We're making sound progress."

"What does Matthew say about that?"

"Matthew had a lot to say." He sauntered over to join her. "Until I decided it was time to pull the lid off our news."

Sucking down a breath, she found his eyes. "You told him we were pregnant?"

"And took great pleasure saying that we're due just before my birthday. I finished by letting him know that even if the baby came late, I would fight him to my last before I'd let him keep that trust." He moved a miniature love seat closer to a window in the dollhouse. "If he decides to have a shoot-out, it could take time and a lot of money. He's an exceptional lawyer with connections everywhere, but I'm sure as hell not going to roll over and play dead."

"Bet he was gobsmacked."

Armand remembered Matthew's reaction—ice-blue gaze clear, his demeanor cool. "Honestly, I think he expected the news—about the baby as well as my challenge."

She moved the love seat back to its original position. "Did he hand in his resignation?"

Armand moved the love seat back. It fit better by the window. "He's not ready to throw in the towel. I might have to go through the process of gaining the support of the other board members and asking him to resign his seat. He can keep his shares, as long as he's denied any executive power."

She straightened the tiny welcome mat at the front of the display. "What a sad way to end a relationship."

Armand studied her thoughtful profile. An easy bet she was thinking about the links she and her mother were rebuilding. He was happy for her, but they both knew reconciliation between Matthew and him was out of the question.

However, while Armand could no longer count on Matthew's friendship, he could, in part, understand the lawyer's motive for betrayal. Armand might have seemed like a nephew or, possibly, a son, but Matthew now had a child of his own to champion and fight for; he'd recognized a once-in-a-lifetime opportunity and seized it.

Dante had taught them both well. Though it pinched in this situation, "loyalty to one's own" was a philosophy Armand had been raised to respect. Blood—pure blood—was always thicker than water. That's the way things were. The way things had to be.

Clenching his jaw, he pushed those thoughts aside. He was home and wanting to enjoy his beautiful wife's company. He looped an arm around her waist and drew her away. The bedroom was calling. "Let's not talk about him. What have you been up to?"

"Studying for my exam."

He frowned and brought her closer as they meandered past an arrangement of stuffed animals. "You should take a rest after that."

He waited. Interesting…she didn't agree but didn't

disagree, either. No doubt the closer the birth got, the less attractive working outside of home must seem. One problem solved.

A thought struck and he stopped to glance back over the room, exactly as they'd seen it in the store, but with some added touches—a clown mobile over the cot, a carousel light on a round corner table.

"What were you doing in here anyway?" A grin chipped at one corner of his mouth.

Smiling, too, she stopped to tug his tie. "I was thinking that before too long, he'll be needing new furniture. They grow quickly."

"Will we use this setup for the next one or try something different?"

She shot him a round-eyed, then adoring look. "How many children would you like?"

He wanted to sweep her up and carry her away. Now, while that priceless look still lit in her eyes. He dropped a kiss on the tip of her perfect nose. "Three sounds like a good number."

She scooped her arms under his and clung to him, burying her cheek against his chest. "I'm so grateful our baby won't be an only child. That he'll have brothers or sisters to play with and love."

He stroked her hair and breathed in her flowery scent while her muffled words both soothed and strangled his heart. Growing up he'd had so much and she had had so little, but neither possessed what was most important—a sense of connection.

In fact, sometimes as a boy he'd felt cleaved in half. Until he'd learned to shut those feelings off. But with this baby on the way, thoughts of siblings, about family—real family—invaded his thoughts more and more. Particularly today at his lawyers'. He'd thought about it so hard, the pen had almost snapped in his hand.

"I wonder if it's true?"

Armand snapped back. "What's true?"

She tipped back to meet his eyes. "Did you know that firstborn siblings are more likely to be leaders and to succeed as leaders?"

Gut clenching, he steered her again toward the door. He'd had enough of nursery musings for one day.

"I looked it up on the Net this morning," she went on. "Some big professor did a study on intelligence. She found that, of over three hundred eminent twentieth century personalities, forty-six percent of them were firstborn children."

He grunted. "Don't know that necessarily applies in this situation."

They'd made it halfway to the train set when she stopped to cough out a laugh. "Why not?"

His jaw shifted. "Why do you think?"

That laugh again. "Armand, if I knew, I wouldn't ask."

The skin around his collar began to heat. Mother of mercy, he didn't need this discussion now. Still, from the curious but determined look in her eyes, he might not be able to avoid it.

And, hell, maybe today was the day for declarations. He could get it off his chest, out in the open, and not have to stew over it a moment more. What was done was done, and that would be the end of it.

He scrubbed his cheek. "The first sibling rule might not apply because they'll have different…" Genes, blood—fathers?

Her soft palm settled against the square of his jaw, over his hand. "Oh, Armand, you don't need to worry."

He held his breath. Surely it wasn't that easy. He had to make himself, and the inescapable facts, clear. "You understand…there'll be a…" He tried to find the right word but came up with only one. "A *difference* between this one and the rest."

She craned up on tiptoe and kissed him, light and sweet. "There won't be any difference. I have no doubt, and neither should you. You'll be as great a father to this child as you will to any that follow. No one will love you any less, I promise."

The almighty knot beneath his ribs threatened to cut off his air. She thought he was worried that this child wouldn't feel for him as deeply as a son would his biological father? Of course, that was possible. After what he'd done today, maybe even probable. But that couldn't be avoided. He'd made a decision as head of the family. He'd signed those papers. That was how it must be!

She sought out and held his hands. "I'm booked in for an ultrasound before my exam. Dr. Fielding said we'll be able to see so much more than last time. She might even say whether she thinks it's a boy or a girl."

He only half heard over the deafening pulse pounding in his head. This situation had to be cleared up. He needed to get it aired and, more important, she needed to understand.

Squeezing her hands, he willed her to focus. "Tamara, I have something to say and I want to say it now. I don't want you to find out later."

Her jaw grew slack and pupils shrank. Then she blinked. "Has Matthew done something—"

"This has nothing to do with Matthew. It's about us, this baby."

She squirmed her hands from his and backed up. "Armand, you're frightening me."

"I signed some papers today. My will." Tamara waited, face ashen. His throat closed over. He could still shut up. Keep quiet until it needed to be said. Perhaps after she'd had the next baby, or the next. But now he'd started, he couldn't stop.

"There's a clause that dictates the limit on this child's inheritance, and a formula to work out how subsequent children will share equally among themselves."

Her palm went to her belly. "Are you saying that you don't want to treat our children equally? That this child won't have equal say in your company and estate?"

"I could have waited until we had another, but I didn't want to leave anything to chance. I need to make certain everyone and everything is looked after properly."

"Like your father should have thought more about you and that stupid clause?"

He shoveled a hand through his hair. Hard to admit, but he said, "Yes."

"And what about the way he looked after Marc?"

The name—the defection it implied—grated more than usual. His voice lowered to a growl. "His name was Marco."

Her expression was pained. "You don't have a right to decide that for him."

Waving a dismissive hand, he spun away, giving her his back. "Don't bother getting defensive with me about him. I offered him a stake in the company, which he refused."

"A wild guess, but maybe because his father disowned him and Marc didn't want any part of it."

"Dante believed Marco was another man's child."

He heard her gasp. "That's rubbish and you know it!"

"Perhaps. But it was what Dante believed." The man had his pride, a company to build, a certain level to maintain. Turning back, Armand slapped his thighs. "What, in God's name, was he supposed to do?"

But Armand knew, even if he kept it locked away: love and nurture the poor kid anyway.

She huffed, an incredulous sound. "If that's your interpretation, you must think you're being pretty darn generous giving this child anything at all." Her slim nostrils flared. "Then again he has served a purpose."

His insides began to churn. Sweat erupted down his spine. "I admit it started out that way. But I did want him to have two parents. I still want him to have every advantage."

"Because of guilt?" she jeered. "Because you had everything and Marc had nothing?"

Armand cursed aloud. "He had our mother."

Blood beginning to boil, he averted his gaze. No. He would *not* go there.

He gathered his wits and any remaining patience. "I want to look after this child. This baby is my blood."

Mistrust and confusion swam in her eyes. "You said you wanted to be his father."

"I do."

"And what kind of father is that? I have a father, too. Rich, apparently, and quite well-known. He might as well be the man on the moon."

He shook his head. "I can't do anything about that."

"Believe me…I don't want or need you to."

He understood that sentiment well enough. When a parent walked away without good reason, at some point, it's too late to redeem what was lost.

Tamara seemed to read his thoughts. "Angela wanted to take you, you know that, don't you? But Dante wouldn't let her."

He held up a hand to cut her off. "She made a choice."

"He made it for her."

"The right choice. She should have listened."

"You're suggesting she should have allowed him to blackmail her into giving up her career in exchange for her family?"

His tolerance evaporated. Time to bring that other issue to a head. "What choice would you have made?"

"I shouldn't have to choose. Angela shouldn't have, either."

"Sometimes there is only one right choice, no matter the sacrifice."

"As long as people like you and your father aren't the ones missing out."

"For God's sake, I just want a family. A happy, structured, traditional family."

"That's what you want?"

His chin kicked up. "More than anything."

She slowly shook her head. "I'll tell you something, Armand. You want *control* more than anything. After this conversation, I don't know if you're even capable of love."

He knew the perfect line. The phrase that could help close this ridiculous widening rift. It would serve his purpose, salve her hurt, yet those three little words stuck in his neck like a bone.

Her expression changed, became almost pitying. "My God, you can't even say it now when it could mean everything. You planned it so carefully. Orchestrated it all so well." A wry smile ticked at the edge of her mouth. "Best laid plans, hey, Armand?"

Her pace picked up as she headed for the door. Adrenaline flooded his system and he lurched forward. "Where are you going?"

"To my former room," she said, still walking, "to do some planning of my own."

She was threatening him?

Voice pitched low, he locked his arms over his chest. "Don't forget, Tamara…we're married and nothing will ever change that." As long as he had breath left in his lungs.

Stopping by the train set, she looked at him hard over one shoulder. "You were hurt growing up and my heart goes out to that child. I get you want to create that happy family you missed out on, but the closer you come to something you don't understand the more you push it away. You're more like your father than you'll ever realize, and I won't hang around to be your trophy wife or incubator. I certainly can't allow my child to be used and hurt to help fulfill your egocentric dynastic dreams."

Eyes bright with unshed tears, she screwed the ruby and wedding rings off her finger and dropped them into the train's coal car. "What goes around, comes around." She flicked a switch.

As the train tooted and chugged out on its loop, Armand prepared to follow her. He wouldn't let her walk away. He must make her see!

But his feet seemed stuck in quicksand while that train zipped around and around and Tamara's parting words echoed through his mind.

Armand slowly crouched and, resting his chin on forearms crossed on the table, stared blankly at the track.

What the hell was he going to do?

CHAPTER TWELVE

ARMAND stood like a zombie at his office window, staring at busy Sydney ferries churning white trails across the harbor's brilliant blue bite far below. They reminded him of Tamara's veil and how she'd looked that day. Then came an image of how she'd looked several days ago when she'd threatened to leave, and that sick, desperate feeling welled up inside him again.

This morning, with Ruth making herself scarce hiding behind the pantry door, he'd questioned Tamara while she'd calmly munched her jam toast. She'd lifted her gaze from the notes she studied for this afternoon's exam, and had confirmed she would indeed be gone tonight. She had the means, which included a stubborn streak, enough money and a mother who wanted to make up for past mistakes. He'd thought Elaine would be on his side. Guess he could think again.

His fist slammed against the windowpane and the *thwack* echoed like a guillotine drop through the room. He'd tried placating her and seducing her, and he'd come close several times to yelling at her, but he knew from experience how well that worked. Still, something would keep her there and, dammit, he *had* to work out what that something was. He needed Tamara, and that need had nothing to do with inheritance. Desire, passion? Yes, but more than that, too.

His gaze fell away from the flocks of seagulls wheeling conflicting circles over the water. He trod to his desk, his legs feeling jet-lagged and brain fuzzy from no sleep.

At first he gazed, uncaring, at the midsized mustard-colored envelope his secretary had brought in a half hour ago to set upon his desk. But now the address seemed to jump out at him—home details, rather than DLE's. His head cocked. The label was addressed to Mr. and Mrs. De Luca. Obviously sent here by mistake.

He snatched up the envelope and flipped it over. Every muscle tensed. "Sender, Dr. Marion Fielding."

He swiped any hint of guilt away. Whatever the envelope contained, it was addressed to them both. He had every right to open it.

He ripped the envelope wide open and, impatient, shook the contents out. After scooping up the yellow DVD case, he read the slip attached. "De Luca ultra-sound" and today's date.

The disc contained images of the baby he and Tamara had talked about and imagined so often.

A wave of prickling heat infused the base of his skull. He scrubbed the back of his hand over his beading brow and steadied himself against the desk.

He needed to view this, and he needed to do it now.

Clicking open the case, he extracted the silver disc and strode across the room to the media corner. The

DVD compartment was entirely too slow whirring out from its console. After pressing the appropriate button, he twirled his wedding band, waiting an eternity for the picture to appear on the widescreen plasma TV.

He'd known Tamara had an appointment this morning. He'd half expected her to say he could shove his expensive medical support. But full credit to her, she hadn't. Despite her anger and disappointment, she still wanted the best for her child. Dammit, he wanted that, too. He wanted that child to have everything, but events had spiraled out of control. He couldn't deliver and the realization was killing him.

The main page flickered up. Armand flexed his hand then pressed Play All.

He zeroed in on the grainy image—a baby...a real baby with toes and eyes and a heart beating like a little frog's. Its legs moved like a spaceman's. He seemed to wave in slow motion. Gaze riveted, Armand sat on the coffee table behind him.

Via the audio, he heard the doctor speaking with Tamara. He expected his wife to sound sad or lost. But her voice was clear, calm and...excited. Maybe a trifle choked up. But he heard little gasps, and when the baby turned as if to face them, a snatch of joyful laughter. When he brought his tiny fist to his mouth, Armand laughed along with them. A little leg kicked out and his mind's eye drew a football sailing through the air. As it arced down, Armand saw himself catching it.

Stinging emotion pressed in behind his nose and eyes. He cleared his throat, but his jaw dropped a little when a paint-box pen wrote letters across the bottom of the screen. In pink: hello, mummy. In blue: hello, daddy. A circle drew around the blue.

A boy?

Joints turned to jelly, Armand caught himself when he fell to one side. As the baby kept kicking and Tamara kept laughing and talking, he pushed up and came slowly nearer. At last truly understanding, he gazed at the amazing image—alive and calling to him—then reached out to touch the flickering screen.

Standing in the late-afternoon light bleeding in through her bedroom's arch window, Tamara forced herself to gaze down at the selection of beautiful clothes strewn across her bed. Setting her jaw, she sniffed, then knocked aside an escaped tear with her fist.

Nothing prevented her from what she must do. She'd completed her exam and knew she'd done well enough to go on to complete her degree this coming semester; she might not be the smartest cookie in the jar, but she was one of the most determined.

Darling Ruth had given her a suitcase for packing and the cab had been ordered. Her mother awaited her flight's arrival in Melbourne. All that remained was to…

All she needed to do was…

Go.

On her way to dig out her jeans from a drawer, she had to stop and bite her quivering lip. Her husband, her hopes for the future, the shining light that held all the promise that dawning love could bring…all over.

She dragged herself back to the suitcase. Lying at her

feet, Master gave a troubled jowl-jostling growl then nudged her ankle with his wet nose. She stooped to ruffle his soft warm ears, then, annoyed at her trembling, but helpless to stop, laid a few items in the open suitcase. Underwear, two day outfits, one pair of mules, classic black trousers, a weensy baby-blue playsuit…

She expelled a sharp breath as an avalanche of insufferable anguish rained upon her. Her quaking knees buckled and she withered onto the lavender quilt, feeling to her very core the sobs about to break.

Her head dropped into her hands. All that trust, wasted. All that love and nowhere to put it.

A familiar flutter in her belly called her attention. She found a soft smile and cupped the mound barely evident beneath her white linen skirt suit. Despite her pain, she had to give thanks for this miracle. How could she forget, even for one second? She had the perfect place to funnel her affection. Here, beneath her palm, lay the reason she must leave this huge empty house. A unique and deserving little person needed to preserve his identity and sense of self-worth. Those lessons couldn't be learned well with Armand De Luca presiding over all, calling her child "son" when what he meant was "pawn."

Gritting her teeth, she pushed to her feet. Be damned if she'd let that happen.

Tossing her cosmetic case in on top of a nightdress, she thought again of her upcoming exit from the De Luca mansion. Armand had come home early. Tamara hoped, despite her warning, he wouldn't try to make her stay. This morning, she'd made it clear that if he interfered, she would contact Matthew and suggest a paternity test, which would throw a huge spanner in Armand's works. She'd made a decision. In exchange for her uncomplicated departure, she would let Armand claim the baby was his legitimate heir, but only for as long as was needed to secure control of DLE.

But no mistake—the twelve-month separation period, which needed to expire before divorce papers were lodged, would begin this very day. When he was old enough, she would explain everything to her child. She prayed he'd understand.

She swung the suitcase off the bed, glancing around one last time as the weight took her arm. She'd already said a teary goodbye to Ruth earlier. Now all that was left was to walk out the door.

She'd crossed to her happy plant to say goodbye when through the window she saw a late-model silver Mercedes swerve up the wide tree-lined drive. Dropping the leaf she held, she moved to gain a better view. The car stopped abruptly and directly below. Matthew Mohill got out, barely allowing time to shut the driver's door before he loped toward the entrance. She couldn't quite make out if he was upset or excited.

Still wondering, she inspected the diamond wristwatch Armand had given as a first-week anniversary gift, then released the catch to set it on top of the figurines' glass cabinet. Her taxi was due soon. In ten minutes she'd be gone.

As she made her way down the sweeping staircase, elevated tones of conversation caught her ear. Matthew's cultured voice drifted up first.

"An interesting game of cat and mouse, Armand, but all good things must come to an end."

Armand's voice rumbled up. "There's only one reason I allowed you into my house and that's to have the pleasure of telling you to go straight to hell."

Still descending, Tamara's steps slowed. She couldn't help but eavesdrop.

"You've played some clever moves," Matthew announced. "I'm not the least surprised. Your father chose the right one."

"Be careful, Matthew. You have no right to use that superior tone when you've cast aside loyalties in order to steal from me."

Matthew spoke as if reciting from a script. "By securing indefinite control of the balance of interest, awarded to my care by the legal and sacred wish of the great Dante De Luca."

Armand's tone was edged with jagged ice. "I'll see someone dead first."

Eyes wide and heart galloping, Tamara drew closer to the main room's entrance, close enough to see Matthew, in a dark pin-striped suit, standing by a large potted palm.

"I remember saying something very similar decades ago," Matthew said, "but to myself. I was fresh out of law school when I helped Dante structure contracts and develop relationships, both private and political, which would help grease palms and win contracts for years to come. Lucrative contracts that held the promise, and eventually did deliver millions."

Long strong legs braced in dark trousers, Armand deliberately crossed his arms and cocked one brow. "You're boring me."

Matthew helped himself to the contents of a crystal scotch decanter, which sat on a drinks trolley near one of two embroidered fabric couches. "We were a partnership, Dante and I. Nobody cares to recall that now. I had the legal expertise, your father had the initial funds." He chuckled as he poured. "We were going to own the world."

Armand's hands went into his pockets. "Your point?"

Matthew set down the decanter and waved his tumbler. "All in good time, my boy." He tasted from the inch of liquor, then tilted his head as if giving it a pass. He eased down in the couch. "After the contracts were in order, Dante decided he didn't need me. He approached the men at the top and cut me out. Oh, he was generous enough to make a place for me within his company. Even gifted me a generous amount of shares when he went public."

Armand's eyes narrowed to slits. "If that's true, why did you stay at DLE?"

Matthew shrugged. "Revenge. One day, I planned to get my own back. Over the years, as I acquired more wealth and prestige within my profession, I lost my thirst for blood. And I genuinely cared for you, my boy. You're everything Dante was, but more."

Matthew wedged back in the cushions and crossed his legs. "Dante had a sturdy heart for business but, sadly, a rather unbalanced one for family. It was wrong to cut Marco off like that, but I never understood quite so well as I do now that I, myself, am to be a father."

Tamara pressed in against the wall, holding her breath as Matthew's pale eyes grew strangely dark.

"Dante and I were partners, but it's much too late to discuss a fifty-fifty split. My child deserves, and will eventually control, the majority share of that company, whether you like it not."

While Matthew calmly sipped his scotch, Armand's black expression shifted. "If all this is true, why did my father put the trust in your name?"

"I played possum for so many decades, I'm sure he thought I no longer carried a dagger. And I'm certain he believed you would act promptly to ensure an heir. You always did as you were told."

Matthew suddenly stilled, frowned and turned his head. Tamara ducked, but he'd already seen her. He waved her in. "Come out, dear girl. Heaven knows, you play a starring role in this charade."

Armand's hands came of his pockets as he drew up to his full intimidating height. "Leave her out of this."

Matthew seemed amused. "Because you care? About her, or the bastard she carries?"

Face a study in blind rage, Armand half scrambled over one couch to get to the other. Tamara ran to block his path, but he growled and almost knocked her flying. "Get out of my way."

She held him. "What's that going to accomplish?"

He picked her up and set her aside. "A broken nose, for starters."

She blocked his path. "And then?"

Armand's ragged breathing eased marginally and his gaze drifted from Matthew to her. He studied her as if through a hazy screen. Then he truly focused and gripped her shoulders. "Tamara, we have to talk."

Setting his tumbler on the coffee table, Matthew piped up. "About paternity matters? Too late. I know the child isn't yours. You're not the only one who makes good use of private investigators, Armand." He unfolded to his feet. "The terms of the will are not met. The trust stays with me. Court adjourned."

Armand's grip, which had slid to Tamara's hand, tightened. "What in the name of Hades makes you think that under any circumstances I'll stand back and let that happen?"

Matthew flicked lint from a jacket sleeve. "You have no legal standing."

"I have rights, and, more importantly, I have my family's interests to protect."

Matthew looked scandalized. "What you have is a woman who sleeps with one man then married his brother, and possibly, if no other man was involved in the meantime, you have a niece or nephew." While Tamara gasped, Matthew darted her a cursory glance. "Sorry to sound so heartless, but we seasoned barristers go for the jugular."

Armand's deep voice was lethal. "Listen to me, Matthew, because I won't say this again. I don't care what your story is. I know only two things. You double-crossed me and I will win controlling interest of De Luca Enterprises if I have to fight you for rest of my days." He stepped closer. "If you think I won't win, by all means try me. And if you speak to my wife like that again, you won't have to worry about DLE. You'll be dead."

While Tamara gazed over at the man who had defended

her like no one else could, the room fell quiet. No ticking clocks or outside noise intruded. The world had been reduced to one fierce blue gaze burning into another.

Matthew backed down first. His gaze slid between the two of them as if assessing their arrangement and his position. "There is one thing we can all three be sure of," he finally said. "You're going to be taken to the cleaners in divorce court." He grinned at Tamara, affecting a slight bow. "Perhaps I could offer you my services."

While she felt physically repulsed, Armand announced, "There won't be a divorce."

Matthew drew a card from his shirt pocket and tossed it toward the coffee table. "Call me. Perhaps we can discuss the benefits of my representation."

Matthew had barely disappeared from the room, and hopefully their lives, before a car horn blared outside.

Tamara's stomach jumped. It was time. "That's my cab." Before she could think any more on it, she moved to collect the case she'd dropped earlier by the room's entrance.

Armand's strong grip on her arm held her back. His voice was a mix of steel and tempting deep velvet. "Don't go."

Arcing around to face him, heartbeat tripping wildly, she tried to wrench free. *Please, Armand, don't make this worse.* "You know I have to." This scene had been difficult enough without prolonging the agony.

His bristled jaw hardened. "I need you."

Her heart squeezed so much she couldn't breathe. She chose to ignore his deeper meaning. "No need to pretend about paternity now. Sounds like you might be in for a real fight."

His grip, still on her upper arm, eased fractionally. The heat of his gaze combed her lips, then her throat. She tingled all over by the time his eyes finally locked again with hers.

"Would you be happy if I lost?"

Her chin tucked in as she coughed out a denial. "Of course not. I don't want to hurt you, Armand. I…"

Swallowing her confession achieved nothing. He said it for her.

"You love me. And I love you, more than I ever wanted to admit."

Her eyes drifted closed as those longed-for words and raw energy seeped in to drug her. His hand traveled down her arm, leaving a series of flash fires in its wake before his fingers curled around to thatch with hers. The vibration of a pulse popping in his wrist hummed through her blood. She should tug away, leave now, but she needed to see this out first.

"Love drove my father crazy," he said. "Love at twenty-four made me want to lie in a big black hole and never come out. But your love, this love, is better than any fairy tale. This is real. We can't lose it."

Emotion, heady and bright, swirled around to lift her up. She tried not to breathe in his scent or fall too deeply into his imploring lidded gaze. Still, the tug of his magnetism was almost too strong to resist.

Her mouth quaked at one corner and heart broke in two as she forced out a strangled whisper. "Armand… it's not enough. It's too late."

Natural heat enveloped her as he brought her near. "Too late for this?"

His kiss was more than it had ever been before—undiluted magic, simmering, sparkling sensations that propelled her soul toward the heavens. The warm palm pressing on the small of her back, his mouth working so beautifully with hers…every screaming, aching part of her wanted to forgive everything, believe, and fall completely under his spell.

But it wasn't that simple. He'd not only stomped on her feelings, he'd dismissed the very foundations upon which she meant to build the rest of her life. Her dream hadn't changed. Nothing could or would come before the best interests of this child. Though she couldn't imagine it now, someday, somewhere, she hoped to find someone who believed in her dream as much as she did. But she would never compromise. She'd rather be alone.

After the kiss trailed away, Armand searched her face. Seeing her resolve, he frowned and tried a different tack.

He rearranged a length of hair back over her shoulder. "I understand why you don't trust me, but this isn't about believing whether I'm willing or able to change." He scratched at the side of his head, cleared his throat. "What I feel, what I know is real between us, is about who I've always been. But that part of me was smothered, almost crushed, beneath a ton of baggage from my past."

He moved his palms to cup her face, imploring her with his eyes to understand. "You've moved on, mending fences with Elaine and already putting aside any grief over the man who didn't acknowledge you."

She tried to shrug away from his compliment, but he stopped her with a finger pressed to her lips.

"Tamara, today I discovered how far I'd come, too." The line between his brows faded. "Let me show you something."

Every cautious cell in her body cried out, warning her not to follow him down any path that might lead to the dangers of renewed seduction. But his words just now—the ones she'd so longed to hear—kept whirling through her mind, pushing her to bend, prodding her to forgive.

Armand's hopeful expression sobered. "Do this and if you still want to go, I'll step aside and never bother you again."

Despite his vow sounding like a death knell, she let her shoulders sag and nodded.

On a mission, he drew her to the television and pressed a couple of buttons. When a picture of her baby flicked up on the screen, Tamara's throat swelled. Somehow a bubble of emotion still managed to squeak out.

Totally entranced by the movements, as she had been earlier that morning, Tamara forgot her company. When she finally did remember, she found that Armand's attention was riveted not on the screen, but on her.

While he faced her, she faced the monitor square on. Cheeks flaming, she compressed her lips then tried to divert his interest back to the images. "How did you get the DVD?"

"Friendly fairies?" He moved closer and she caught the grin crinkling the corners of his eyes. "It was delivered to my office instead of here."

With great effort, she tugged her gaze away from the purpose blazing in his to watch her little man suck his thumb. She smiled, remembering her burst of happiness when Marion had confirmed she believed it was a boy.

Tamara tipped her chin. "Didn't you want to watch this?"

"I'd hoped we might be able to catch it again later."

His arms wrapped around her waist and the semihard exterior of her resolve warped like a mirage as warmth poured over and through her. Her huge day, this big screen, Armand's overwhelming charm kidnapping her all over again...

Tears, born of confusion and forbidden desire, flooded her eyes. She couldn't cope with anything more.

His breath stirred the hair at her ear. "That's our child. No matter what happens, I'll always look after him."

While she held herself tight and gazed with loving eyes at her baby, he moved closer still.

"You'll be pleased to know this afternoon I had my lawyers destroy that will," he said. "If you'd like, we can go together and make sure everything is exactly as it should be in the next, whether we own a billion dollars or ten cents." His lips brushed her hair while his hot woodsy scent tantalized her senses. "I'd be happy with nothing as long as I have the two most important people in my life."

Clogged up and unable to speak for stupid desperate hope, she blinked and two salty drops rolled down each cheek.

He groaned. "I love you, Tamara. Adore you. And there are only two things you can do about it. Walk out that door—or trust me." He pressed in extra close so his chest wedged up against her shoulder and his deep rich voice washed over her. "Please, trust me."

Her resolve shook, almost toppled, but one question still burned bright. Avoiding his eyes, she studied the white knuckles of her clasped hands. "What if I decide to relaunch my business?"

She was almost finished with her degree and she'd always meant to apply her knowledge in a practical way. She couldn't foresee the future, but neither could she see herself giving up that goal.

He shrugged. "Then I'd have added reason to get serious about sharing the responsibilities of child care, which I intend to initiate as soon after the birth as possible."

Heartbeat crashing at her ribs, she tossed him a dumbfounded glance. "You're kidding me."

His brow buckled, but his eyes twinkled. His hands on her hips, he pivoted her around to face him. "I confess, I'm not so convinced about dirty diaper changes, but I'm in for everything else. I want to do the parties, and the homework, and the aches and pains, and football practice." His thumb and crooked finger caught her chin and tilted it up. "You believe me, don't you, Tamara? You have to, because I've never meant anything more in my life. Nothing will ever be more important to me than you and our family…every member, everyone equal, everyone loved."

As he moved to gather her in, she found a kernel

of courage and arched a brow. "I'm still not wholly convinced."

He blinked and pulled back. "You're not?"

She fanned her hands over his white shirtfront then tugged the loosened knot of his tie toward her. "Maybe I should test-drive some of this new you before I make up my mind?"

Grinning, he bundled her in. "Sounds good. Let's start in low gear."

He dropped a series of exquisitely light, incredibly right kisses on first her top, then bottom lip, then each corner of her mouth until she discovered her arms were threading round his neck and she was kissing him back, enjoying his caress more and more each soul-lifting moment.

When they finally surfaced, she felt as if her feet hovered inches off the ground. Her hands winged around from behind his neck to cup each side of his jaw. She couldn't hold it back a moment more. "I love you, Armand. I've wanted to tell you for so long."

He blinked several times, his smile soft with gratitude, gaze intense and clear. He pressed a kiss to her temple before he tucked her head under his chin. "If you want another test run, I'm available the rest of the day. In fact, the rest of your life."

Overflowing with joy and hope and so much love, she moved to gaze up at her husband's handsome face. "I'm thinking we should start right about now."

He smiled before his head lowered again. "Amen to that."

EPILOGUE

TAMARA eased out a satisfied sigh as her gaze ran over the Happy Birthday banner that spanned her kitchen's archway. A year already. Where had the time gone?

A hand on her arm broke Tamara's thoughts.

Hair set in a stylish chignon, Elaine smiled. "Quick, sweetheart. Ruth's bringing out the cake."

Tamara dimmed the lights before they moved together to a large timber table. Looking relaxed in blue jeans and T-shirt, Armand stood blowing a party whistle while his son bounced in a highchair, squealing with delight. When Tamara joined him, Armand automatically wrapped an arm around her waist. A moment later, Ruth set down a cake, topped with a single sparkler that rained shooting stars.

Ruth thrust both hands into her apron pocket. "There you go, little man. A great big one today!"

The four adults broke into song while Maxem De Luca beamed and clapped his dimpled hands.

On the last of three cheers, Armand dropped a kiss on the toddler's crown then gently ruffled the toffee-colored curls. As Elaine helped Ruth cut the cake, he swept his wife close and smiled into her adoring eyes. "Looks like Maxem got his wish."

Tamara laughed. "You put in the request for chocolate cheesecake, not Max."

"I was talking about the swing set." He inspected the palm of one hand. "Took half the night putting that monster together."

She kissed his palm where the spanner had worn a blister. "You could've paid someone to fit it."

He nuzzled close. "Now, where's the fun in that?"

The kitchen extension rang. As Ruth crossed to answer it, Armand leaned over to collect two plates and hand one to his wife. "Whoever it is, Ruth, I'm unavailable."

Everyone was seated, the lights switched back up, when Ruth reappeared. Armand stopped feeding Maxem as she offered him the phone. Ruth's voice was grave. "You might want to take this."

On the other side of the table, Elaine took over feeding duties while Armand listened, frown growing deeper. By the time he disconnected, Tamara was knotted up inside. This was it.

She clasped her hands in her lap. "Your lawyer?"

Armand nodded before he arched a wry brow and grinned. "Seems Matthew Mohill has finally backed down."

The breath Tamara held came out in a whoosh. "Oh, thank God."

Armand covered both her hands and squeezed. "Might have something to do with his own boy's birthday this week, but Matthew apparently wants to end the war and simply get on with his life."

Tamara's thoughts jumped ahead. "Then all systems are go with China?"

Armand winked. "Next week the interim contracts can be replaced with something more permanent." He scooped up the whistle and blew at Maxem, who squealed as if it were a brand-new game.

While congratulations and thanks were lobbed back and forth across the table, Tamara pressed her lips together. She'd planned to tell her husband in private but now, this moment, seemed the best time to make her announcement. "I have some news of my own."

Elaine looked over expectantly. "You've decided to do more study?"

Armand guessed next. "You want to restart your business? We'll keep each other busy, won't we, son?" He tickled Maxem's tummy and the baby grabbed his index finger and shook it like a hand.

"Both wrong." Tamara's heart felt set to burst. "We're going to be parents again. Max is going to have a baby brother or sister."

The room fell silent. Even Maxem sat still, bright blue eyes wide and waiting. Then Armand sprang to his feet, scooping Tamara up along on the way. He twirled her around so her feet arced through the air. When he set her gently down, he speared a hand through his hair. "Why didn't you tell me?"

Out of breath, she laughed. "I just did."

His contented gaze probed hers. "Soon we'll have a Georgia."

"Or Daniela. Or another little boy." She shrugged. "Doesn't matter which."

The crook of his finger trailed her cheek. "I love you so much. Don't think I've told you today."

Throat thick with emotion, she softly smiled. "It was the first thing you said when you woke up this morning."

"And the last thing I'll say before we sleep tonight."

"Da-dad." They both stopped to look. Maxem stretched forward, holding out his arms.

Armand's lips brushed hers. "Hold that thought," he murmured. "I'll definitely be back."

As Tamara watched him slip Maxem from the high-chair, chuckling as he held his son high, she hugged herself and silently gave thanks. Miracles came in all shapes and sizes. Big and small, she cherished both of hers more and more each day.

Three Latin males, brothers, must take brides...

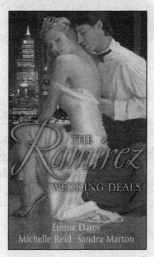

Let these three sexy brothers seduce you in:

THE RAMIREZ BRIDE
by Emma Darcy

THE BRAZILIAN'S BLACKMAILED BRIDE
by Michelle Reid

THE DISOBEDIENT VIRGIN
by Sandra Marton

Available 1st May 2009

THE ROYAL HOUSE OF KAREDES

Two crowns, two islands, one legacy

Volume One
BILLIONAIRE PRINCE, PREGNANT MISTRESS
by Sandra Marton

Wanted for her body – and her baby!

Aspiring New York jewellery designer Maria Santo has come to Aristo to win a royal commission.

Cold, calculating and ruthless, Prince Xander Karedes beds Maria, thinking she's only sleeping with him to save her business.

So when Xander discovers Maria's pregnant, he assumes it's on purpose. What will it take for this billionaire prince to realise he's falling in love with his pregnant mistress…?

Available 17th April 2009

M&B

MILLS & BOON®
Pure reading pleasure™

2 FREE

BOOKS AND A SURPRISE GIFT!

We would like to take this opportunity to thank you for reading this Mills & Boon® book by offering you the chance to take TWO more specially selected titles from the Modern™ series absolutely FREE! We're also making this offer to introduce you to the benefits of the Mills & Boon® Book Club™—

 ★ FREE home delivery
 ★ FREE gifts and competitions
 ★ FREE monthly Newsletter
 ★ Exclusive Mills & Boon Book Club offers
 ★ Books available before they're in the shops

Accepting these FREE books and gift places you under no obligation to buy, you may cancel at any time, even after receiving your free shipment. Simply complete your details below and return the entire page to the address below. You don't even need a stamp!

YES! Please send me 2 free Modern books and a surprise gift. I understand that unless you hear from me, I will receive 4 superb new titles every month for just £3.19 each, postage and packing free. I am under no obligation to purchase any books and may cancel my subscription at any time. The free books and gift will be mine to keep in any case.

P9ZED

Ms/Mrs/Miss/Mr ....Initials ....

BLOCK CAPITALS PLEASE

Surname ....

Address ....

....

....Postcode..

Send this whole page to:
UK: FREEPOST CN81, Croydon, CR9 3WZ